When Deanne Adams is not writing her own stories, she is helping others discover theirs as a story coach and mentor. *The Heretic's Servant* is her first novel.

https://bestbookyoucan.com
https://deanneadams.com

THE HERETIC'S SERVANT

DEANNE ADAMS

authors
AND CO.

For Jenny and William

Also, thanks to Hazel Hitchins for her unstinting support and patient listening;

To Abigail Horne of Authors & Co for her generosity and belief;

To Kat Clarke for her cheerleading;

And to Nick Horton for his cooking, plus his technical advice on carpentry and medical matters. Any errors in this novel are my own because I wasn't listening properly.

CHAPTER ONE

I used to think it started the Christmastime that never was. But really it started years before that. Before the children were born. Before Kate was married. Before we were heretics.

It started when Alice died.

1558: Sherbourne Manor

We prayed. At all hours of the day and night, we prayed. We especially prayed to the patron of sick children, Saint Hugh of Lincoln. Whoever could be spared from the girls' sickrooms was sent to the chapel to raise their pleas to Heaven.

Father Makepeace came up from the church to hear confessions in the family chapel, to root out the neglected sin that had brought punishment on the house. He heard Lord Henry Sherbourne and his wife, my mistress. All the servants were called to him too, the men and then the women, and he urged us to scour every misdeed, every crime of thought from our souls.

My mother tapped me on the shoulder while I was praying

and nodded at the entrance to the small antechamber. I was to make my confession after her, it seemed. I had expected Cook to be sent in next. So did I now outrank Cook? I would have been happy to be the lowliest maid if I could delay being sent to face Father Makepeace and God. I scarcely knew which frightened me more.

I went in directly, not to keep the priest waiting. I fixed my eyes on my clasped hands. Not that I had a secret to hide, you understand. No more than usual – the odd pilfered apple from the larder. I was always hungry at that age. But I knew what was at stake. Father Makepeace did not usually hear servants' confessions here in the house. We went to the church. Kate and Alice must be in mortal danger for him to take this trouble. If Father Makepeace was raking through the entire household in search of the cause of the red plague, then he must be seeking out a great many sins, or else a truly dreadful crime. What if it was me? Had I wished evil upon a fellow creature and forgotten? Or was a stolen apple or two a serious matter of the soul?

"How many times have you stolen apples, Molly? Since your last confession, I mean," Father Makepeace said.

"Twice," I said. "No – three times, I think."

I glanced up into his eyes, and immediately wished I hadn't. They were pale grey and icy sharp. I cast my gaze downwards again.

"Theft is a sin, as you well know," he said. "And a repeat offence too."

I nodded miserably.

"Caused by greed, in this case."

Again I nodded.

"Are you truly sorry? Do you truly mean to control yourself from this time on?"

"Yes, Father." I was sorry. I really was. And I did.

"Do you have anything else to confess?" he asked.

"I don't believe so, Father."

He did not speak immediately so I was compelled to look up. His penetrating gaze saw every thought I'd ever had, I was sure of it. My cheeks grew hot.

"You don't believe so?" he asked. One eyebrow lifted slightly.

"I mean, I can't remember anything else I've done. But I might have done it."

"Done what?"

"I don't know. What if I've done something terrible and now I've forgotten I did it but I still did it and I ought to tell you about it but I can't?"

Father Makepeace pinched the bridge of his nose and closed his eyes. He absolved me of my apple thefts, and I began to feel foolish.

Maybe my confession made a difference. Maybe it didn't. Perhaps Alice was doomed anyway. But perhaps the weight of an apple saved Kate.

The girls did everything together, went everywhere together, even shared their bed still, despite being twelve. They begged their mother not to put them into separate rooms, and she relented. Now they had the smallpox together.

Alice was moved to a bed in another room to give us space to nurse them both. Despite the separation, their illnesses were mirror images. Even young Doctor Phillips remarked on how close their symptoms and responses to treatment were. The crisis of Alice's fever began just an hour after Kate's. They both yelled out in pain and sweated in their fevered sleep. Yet Kate's fever broke, while Alice died as the sun rose.

It should have been me who told Kate about Alice. The household were laying her sister to rest in the family's vault beneath the church. My mother had taken me to one side to tell me I was to stay behind. Alice's sickroom needed putting to rights and airing before the family returned, she said. "Lady Sherbourne cannot bear much more," she told me with a side-long glance at our mistress, who stood waiting, straight-bodied, for Alice to be brought downstairs in her coffin.

I looked too. Lady Sherbourne's features were composed. I didn't see what my mother meant. She must have seen an argument brewing in my face and cut it off sharply before it could leave my mouth. She dug her fingers into my elbow and pulled me farther away from the funeral procession that was forming.

"She is about to do the most painful thing any mother ever must," my mother told me fiercely. "When she returns home, she is not to find any hint of Alice's illness. Am I clear, Molly?"

Now that I looked again at Lady Sherbourne, she had tight lines around her eyes that had not been there a week ago, and I saw that her uprightness was not her usual elegance, like that of a slender ash or beech tree, but the unbending brittleness of a January icicle. She might have shattered at any moment.

For the first time in my young life, I felt something other than duty for Lady Sherbourne. I resolved to do all I could to make this day less painful, even if that meant not going to church to say goodbye to a girl I had grown up serving. The village folk would turn out to line the path to the church door, and I knew that although she felt ready to crumble not one of those people would be able to say that Lady Sherbourne even trembled. My respect for her blossomed into awe.

They left the house at a solemn pace. Father Makepeace led the way in his finest vestments, followed by our four smartest male servants bearing the coffin. Behind Alice walked Lord and Lady Sherbourne. She rested her hand lightly on her husband's arm, holding her thickly veiled head high. My mother fell in close behind her, all watchfulness. The rest of the household followed on. I watched them down the narrow footpath that led to the church until they disappeared around the trees.

I tiptoed around the house that afternoon. Dust motes drifted lazily in the sun-shafts that came through the open windows into the hall. I watched the sun creep across the sky, willing it to move faster until I might expect the family to return from the long service for the dead. The place was strange in the silence. I told myself I didn't like being alone, but I knew what I really feared was that Kate would wake while I was alone with her.

I cleaned the room where Alice had died that morning and stripped all the linen. I swept up the herbs and rose petals and aired the room. Just a lingering cloying sweetness betrayed that someone had been unwell there. I was thinking how grown up I must be for my mother to trust me with the house and Kate, when from outside Kate's room I heard her whimper. Turning in her sleep, I hoped. Dragged back to the reality of being only thirteen, I pushed the door a crack, just enough to peer into the gloom. Her eyes were closed, I thought, and I began to pull the door to. But then she whispered my name.

There was nothing else for it. I opened the door enough to slip through, stepping as lightly as I could. I wondered how lucid she was. Perhaps she would not understand much yet. I went to her side and bobbed my curtsey. It was too dark after the brightness of the landing to make out her features clearly. She could probably see better, and I tried to arrange my face to hide my nerves. I put my hand to her forehead. It was quite cool.

Kate tried to speak again, but only a rasp came out. The beer jug on the low table was becoming visible out of the gloom and I poured a small cupful for her, holding it and propping her up so she could sip. When she had drunk, she sank back onto her pillow.

Kate sighed heavily once, twice. I waited for her to speak but hoped she wouldn't, that she would close her eyes and go back to sleep. A short while and surely the family would be back from church. The clock had struck twice since they had been gone.

"Molly," she said. "It's very dark in here. Open the curtains, will you?"

Fear twisted my voice, threatening to give something away. "I don't know that I should, Miss," I said, grasping for an excuse. "Doctor Phillips didn't say I could."

"Is Doctor Phillips here, Molly?" she asked. I shook my head. "Then he won't know," she said. Her voice already held a shadow of her usual mischief. I was torn between anguish at being unable to prevent her from discovering what had happened, and joy at this sign of her recovery.

Besides, I wasn't being strictly truthful. The doctor hadn't implied that the sickroom had to be kept as it had been during Kate's danger period. He had just said that she must rest. I was a coward, clutching at straws.

My eyes had adjusted to the gloom. The scabs of the smallpox were somehow more obscene now she was looking at me. Not too many on her face, thank God. Hardly any more than I had myself from when I was struck with it a few summers ago. She would get used to them in time. But her pretty hands had fared badly. She would see them immediately in the daylight. That would be bad enough. And once she knew how close she had come, she would ask about Alice.

I didn't move from the bedside.

Kate gave me her sweet smile. That wasn't spoiled, at least. "Just a little fresh air, Molly. It's stifling." I still hesitated. "Go on," she said.

Her gaze was on me. It was irresistible, though she didn't know it. I resigned myself to what was to come. I wanted my mother here. She would have managed this better – probably even fat old Cook would have done better – but I would have to do my best. Perhaps this was my punishment. Or a test.

I went to the window as slowly as I could, hoping for a miracle, for the front door to open and feet to traipse into the hallway. I could rush downstairs to welcome the funeral party home and whisper in Lady Sherbourne's ear that her daughter was awake and on the mend, thank God.

It didn't happen. I loosened the curtains and opened the window to the summer air. The room looked over the path that came from the church. I willed the household to round the bend.

Behind me, Kate gasped. I sucked in a breath and held it. Slowly I turned to face her.

Kate was staring at her hands, covered with crusted scabs the size of peas, turning them over and over. Then she raised them slowly and explored her face. Her breath grew ragged and she began to wail. The sound unglued my feet from the floor. I was by her side in a moment.

"I know, Miss, I know," I said. "But they're not so bad, honest they're not."

Her mouth was open and her eyes stretched wide, silently calling me a liar. Her marked fingers trembled against her nose, cheeks and chin. The wail broke into loud sobs.

"Really, you don't have very many, not there, I promise," I said, taking her hands away from her cheeks. "It could be worse, much worse, Miss." I shut up when my mind caught up with my tongue. Yes, it could have been worse. For Alice it had been.

Kate took great, heaving gulps of air between sobs. I stood frozen like the fool I was, still holding her fingers gently. But then she held out her arms to me and I understood what to do. I sat on her bed and rocked her like I would a tiny child, even though she was only a year my junior.

She cried hard for several minutes. I stroked her hair as if she were my youngest sister. When I lived at home Lizzy always came to me for comfort, not to our aunt. I missed Lizzy. I still saw her at church every week but it was not the same as being there.

Kate calmed at last and let me release her. I smiled at her and told her she was still beautiful, not to worry. She seemed to take comfort from that. It was not her vanity at stake – she had never been vain about her looks. Kate had seen people on the estate and in the village who had not survived smallpox lightly. It was a pity to see their disfigured faces and to know that *they* knew everyone stared at them and nobody would want to marry them. It was hard to know where to look.

I could look more openly at the blacksmith's son. As well as scarring him, the red plague had turned him blind. On sunny days he sat outside his father's forge, face turned to the sun. When I was a little girl living in the village I was fascinated by him. I always stopped to stare and my aunt would have to pull me away. As I grew older I began to wonder whether the young man knew how ugly he had become, and whether it was a curse or a mercy that he was blind.

Then there were those in the churchyard. And now there was Alice.

I took a clean linen square from the table, wiped my own

eyes with the corner, and dabbed her eyes dry, taking care not to knock the sores. "There now," I said, "will you take some more drink?"

Kate nodded and I raised the cup for her to sip again. I began to feel I was doing a good job after all. But she faced me rather than drinking and I saw a question forming in her eyes. I brought the cup closer, quite firmly, to stop the words. She drank but her gaze kept flickering up at me. I tried to smile but it came out wrong. I took a deep breath and focused on stopping my chin from wobbling.

"Can you manage some broth, Miss?" I asked as soon as she stopped drinking. "I know there is some prepared in the kitchen." My voice was too bright. I never was a good dissembler. Without waiting for Kate to answer, I stood up and started moving quickly towards the door.

Her voice stopped me in my tracks before I could reach it. "Where is everyone, Molly?" she said. I turned to face her reluctantly. My mouth opened and closed like I was a landed fish. Kate was suddenly fully alert. "Molly? Why are we alone?" she repeated, more firmly this time.

"They're not here, Miss," I said.

She waited a long time for me to answer differently. Or it might have been a few seconds. Tears pricked at my eyes. I said, "I'm not meant to say, Miss. They – everyone is out." I felt my cheeks redden at the poor excuse and the wobble in my voice.

Kate's brow creased. "Out? Out where?"

"Oh, Miss, I can't say!" I said, crying in earnest now. "They hoped you would sleep longer, until they were home!" I stopped talking abruptly and cursed my own stupidity, determined to say no more even if I were turned away from the house. As if anyone was concerned enough about what I said or did, that day of all days.

"Molly," Kate said. "Where is Mother? Father? Alice? Where are they?"

A knock came at the chamber door. I jumped. They must have returned while I was comforting her. I moved quickly to throw a shawl over Kate's thin shift and went to open the door.

Father Makepeace was framed in the doorway. He was still wearing his ceremonial vestments, grand, yet dark and solemn. I stood back, catching my sobs in my throat. He observed us both with his head tilted, curious.

"You have been spared, Miss Katherine," he said eventually. "You should be on your knees and giving thanks." He glanced sideways at me in silent enquiry. I shook my head and pressed my lips together hard.

He came into the room. Thank goodness. I was spared breaking the worst part of the news to Kate. And who better to tell her than our priest? What better proof of God's mercy than this? I bowed my head in thanks.

Father Makepeace fixed his eyes on Kate and said, "I have news for you, Miss, regarding your sister. She is –" he paused momentarily "– most fortunate."

I opened my eyes and frowned. What on earth could he mean? Surely he did not mean to pretend Alice was well? Father Makepeace's expression was a peculiar one, not the sort one would expect on the face of a man bringing terrible news. I took a few moments to name the emotion. He was – excited.

Kate began to smile. She looked toward me, but whatever was on my face shut down her smile and she turned back to the priest.

"She has been called home to God," Father Makepeace said. He gazed at her evenly. "It is His will."

Kate gasped. Her eyes widened in shock, then her face seemed to collapse. But it was *his* face at that moment that I will never forget. His eyes glittered. A tiny smile pulled at his mouth.

He was not yet satisfied and so he continued, "Your parents brought her to church for burial. She needs your prayers to help her enter Heaven, not your tears. And you must pray for your own salvation too. Let these marks upon you remind you always that your own soul is in constant peril."

Kate pulled the shawl closer to her, hiding her hands. I watched him watching her. I saw him without his mask of holiness. Like a raven at a corpse.

CHAPTER TWO

December 1578: Spicer Hall

Everywhere I went it was as though another servant was trying to get in my way. If it was not one of our usual household, it was one of the extra hands brought in from the village. Large as the house was, I felt it might burst at the seams with all the bodies moving around in it, fetching, carrying, cleaning, washing. Every day, Cook – normally a kind enough woman – made one girl or another cry for being clumsy or not quick enough. The errand boys learned to stay out of reach of her hard hand, and out of her kitchen entirely if they could help it.

It had been like this for two weeks and I was exhausted. Kate's parents were visiting for the Christmas season. Kate was tired too from giving her attention to every tiny detail. Her husband, Sir Edward Spicer, had brought home a deer from the hunt to be dressed and hung. A great deal of noise he and the other men made about it when they presented it to Kate, too. The master's job done, Edward spent much of the time in his study to avoid getting in Kate's way.

I saw Ned more than usual while the preparations were being made. Edward released him from most of his normal duties so that we could have him for the heaviest jobs. A couple of the village girls took to following him around. He told me about it with a wink.

"They don't mean no harm, Moll," he said.

I did not change my expression. "Harm or no, they've no business to."

I took a leaf from Cook's book. I might have needed every strong girl I could get, but I could still pay a visit to the parents of any who got ideas. The warning was enough. They stopped their simpering and hopefully complained about me to the others.

Kate gave Jane – her eldest, named for Lady Sherbourne – tasks to school her to run her own household one day. Messages to pass on, decisions regarding sauces, how much holly to order Old Ned to gather from the woods, that sort of thing. Kate congratulated her on her judgement every time, then gave me the nudge to put the order right.

Harry was seven and named for his grandfather, Lord Henry. Sir Edward had engaged a private tutor that autumn to educate him at home, one Master Greene just come down from Oxford, his first teaching job. When Harry was not in the school-room, he would come to find me, or Jane, or his mother, or even Cook, anyone who would play with him and listen to him chatter. We did not have time to play in those weeks before Christmas. I wished later that we had. Harry would find us and we would pretend to sweep him out of the room with a broom or offer him a treasure we found in our pockets to bribe him to amuse himself elsewhere.

Little Isabel – named purely for herself – was still toddling everywhere and grabbing everything. Whenever she saw her mother she forgot to use her words and screamed to go to her. It upset Kate to have to say no when she was busy, especially since Isabel then screamed all the louder. During the preparations for Christmas, Margaret kept Isabel mainly in the nursery, out of everyone's way. Kate went to see her every day.

It took three days to prepare the best guest room for Lady Sherbourne. First day, it was swept and aired, and two of our extra girls took all the soft furnishings outside for a beating. Then they lit a fire to remove the damp from the air. Lady Sherbourne felt her rheumatism and both Kate and I would feel the rough edge of her tongue if her room were unhealthy. The third day, I polished the furniture myself. These village girls' attempts would not have satisfied.

Finally, a few hours before Lord and Lady Sherbourne's arrival, I brought in a bowl of dried rose petals for the table, made up the bed with the best sheets, and studied the room.

Kate came in. "Finished, Molly?"

"I think so, madam," I said. "Final inspection."

She joined me in studying every corner and nook, fiddling with her wedding ring as she always did when nervous. The curtains of the bed hung slightly uneven and she twitched them so they matched. Kate had wanted to purchase new ones, but Sir Edward had said no. The curtains were still good, he said. He was right. They must have cost a pretty penny. They were new with the house, less than twenty years old. A little sun-faded, to be sure, but quality like this was made to last.

I said as much to Kate.

"I know," she said. "It's just... my mother."

This was true. "Your Lady Mother knows the value of goods," I said. "This room is lovely."

Kate nodded but still worried at the ring on her finger.

I tried to think of something to distract her from Lady Sherbourne's judgement. The room was clean, comfortable, and as richly furnished as any of the family rooms. If Kate's mother came here to criticise, she would find a way to do it regardless. It was easy enough for me to think this, I suppose. It wasn't my mother who was coming.

Kate peeked out of the window. It was too early to start looking out for them, even if they had left Sherbourne Manor at daybreak. Their house was the other side of Rysham, and then a few miles more. I could not think of anything distracting to say but I was saved by Jane's voice on the landing. "Mother?" she called, her quick, light footsteps approaching the room.

The door opened. Jane tumbled in. "Must you run, Janey?" Kate said. "You know you shouldn't."

"I forgot," said Jane. She frowned hard, as she always did when she forgot to be a lady.

Kate's brow relaxed and she smiled at Jane's anxious little face, so like her own. "Don't forget when your grandmother arrives," she said, and stroked her daughter's cheek.

"I won't. Promise." Jane sniffed the fragranced air. "Grandmother will like her chamber, won't she?" she asked.

"Of course. Rose petals are her favourite," Kate replied with confidence, although her eyes darted around the room once more. They came to rest on a tiny, dusty cobweb in the fireplace, billowing in the warm air. She pointed it out to me. "Grandmother will like it very well. Now let's look at your grandfather's chamber. You can be the mistress, and judge of Molly's work in there."

Jane giggled and took her mother's hand, leading the way from the room. Kate cast one more fleeting look around from the doorway. I found a rag in my pocket and removed the offending cobweb.

Lord and Lady Sherbourne's brand-new coach rumbled up the drive just as the church clock struck four. Harry had been outside looking for it every five minutes since two, when his tutor had released him early from the schoolroom.

Master Greene had taken his degree only a few months before and was still a very young man. I remember him as quite a small person, not yet come into the full breadth of a man. He stroked his beard when anyone spoke to him, in what I suppose he thought conveyed the intelligence of his reply. It always made me notice how thin and patchy his beard still was. Not like Ned's.

"The boy has been wriggling on his stool all morning," Greene told me from the half-landing. "If I thought a beating would make that boy learn today, I would have thrashed him soundly." He tried to growl menacingly but he couldn't keep his pitch low. My lips twitched.

Greene didn't fool me for a moment. I looked from his booted feet to his packed travelling bag near the front door and then to his face. I raised an eyebrow. He had the decency to blush, at least. I knew his father. Just a well-off butcher from Rysham with ambition. And I remembered our Master Greene when he was Little Freddie held firmly by his mother's hand.

"Master Greene," I said when he reached the hall. "Of course you want to be off to your family. I don't think anyone blames you for that." I had a whole speech ready about humility and not letting an education turn his head, but he was already the colour of radish skin so I let him off. "Please remember me to your mother."

I gave him his hat and cloak and he scurried out to his horse, which Ned was holding for him.

Once his tutor was safely gone, Harry came out from wherever he had been hiding. From then on, he ducked in and out of doors, letting the heat out of the house. When he was inside he got under my feet or wandered into Kate's parlour, interrupting the reading she and Jane were engaged in. He had a knack for finding whoever of us was busiest at any particular moment. We shooed him away only to find him begging Cook for biscuits in the kitchen a minute later. When Harry wasn't doing that, he was checking the road for the first glimpse of his grandfather's glamorous new coach. Kate told him that watching the road would not bring his grandfather any sooner but he kept going out anyway. He found Old Ned out there to babble at too.

Harry did not usually bother with Ned's father. Old Ned scowled a lot, although that was mainly down to toothache. He was working alone outside that day so Harry didn't have a choice of conversation partner. It was funny to see him bouncing up and down around Old Ned and chattering away, and the old man being as deaf to him as he was to everyone else, except Sir Edward. Old Ned always heard what Kate's husband said with no trouble. After a good while, he finished tidying the grounds and stomped off to the stables to feed the horses, leaving Harry to talk to himself while he wandered up and down the drive as far as the road that led to the village.

The sun was very low when Harry burst into the entrance hall, shouting, "They're here! They're here!" I jumped and spilled some of the mulled ale I was taking to Kate's parlour.

"What have your parents told you about shouting indoors, Master Harry?" I scolded him.

"But Molly, they are here!" Harry repeated urgently, in an only slightly quieter voice. "I saw the coach lamps swinging on the village road. They're here." He hopped from one foot to the other. I couldn't help but smile.

Sir Edward stepped out from his private study off the hallway the next moment, closely followed by Ned. Harry grinned at them, just remembered to salute his father politely, then ran to his mother's room. "Mother! Jane!" he called as he ran. "Come out! They're here!"

Sir Edward chuckled. "You will wake the dead before long, sirrah!" he called to the boy's back. Ned laughed too and caught my eye. I smiled more broadly, and not because of Harry. They laughed harder when Harry reappeared, pulling Kate along by one hand while she tried to straighten her hood with the other. Jane came behind. "Well done, lad," Sir Edward said. "I shall give you a ha'penny."

Margaret, little Isabel's nurse, was negotiating the staircase with Isabel's leading strings in one hand. Isabel was clutching her cloth doll and bumping down the stairs on her behind. She tried to bump faster when she saw her mother at the bottom of the flight, but her skirts tangled further with every bump. "Mamma!" she called and held out her arms.

Kate lifted Isabel down the last few stairs, kissed her, and set her on her feet. "You do look beautiful, dear," she said. "Margaret has dressed you very nicely." The nursemaid and I smoothed the layers of skirts into place again, while Isabel pulled a face and wriggled.

"Remember to be a good girl. Be quiet," Kate added, and

kissed the little girl's cheek again. I reinforced Kate's command. I bent down, looked into Isabel's eyes and placed my finger on my lips. Isabel frowned severely. She copied me, pouting her lips and jamming a pudgy forefinger to them. She kept the finger there very firmly as if this might keep her words contained more securely and I had to hold in a laugh.

Kate was checking the appearance of Jane and Harry and twisting her wedding ring. Her nerves had been growing all afternoon. At least the reading lesson in the parlour meant that Jane had not had the opportunity to get dirty, and her hair was fairly neat under her hood. Harry was passable, for Harry. He was rather pink in the cheeks but his breeches and hose looked cleaner than usual. Kate made a futile effort to tame his hair. "You too, Harry," she said. "Don't speak unless you are spoken to."

Sir Edward coughed gently and offered his hand to Kate in a formal manner. An amused smile pulled at the corners of his mouth. I helped her rearrange her skirts, and she took Edward's hand. "You look lovely, Kate," he told her.

He was right. She did. I don't know that she believed him. She bit her lip. "Thank you, but... *Katherine*, you remember, Edward?" she said.

He raised an eyebrow at her.

"I mean, you remember, *sir*?" she corrected, and smiled at both herself and him.

Harry hopped into his place behind them, then Jane, then I helped Margaret with Isabel, holding her other hand. Ned opened the front door for our little procession to go and greet the guests. He gave me that look as I passed him – the one he gave only me. He put the door on the latch and joined my side.

We reached the carriage sweep just as the liveried manser-vant brought the smart new carriage to a halt. The shining lanterns either side of his box seat twirled one way and then the other. He jumped from his seat and opened the door for Kate's father to step out.

Lord Henry Sherbourne carried his years well, despite being at least sixty. His beard was entirely grey now, yet well-kept. It gave him an air of authority – or perhaps it just suited the authority that was his own. He was still strong and broad, though he climbed out of the coach rather stiffly.

Harry peered around his father at his grandfather, who grinned and winked at his young namesake as he handed Lady Jane out of the carriage. Kate's mother stepped down even more stiffly than he had. She was an angular woman, unusual for a lady well past fifty. She carried herself in the same unyielding way as twenty years ago. Her mouth was firmly unsmiling.

Kate dropped a low curtsey to her parents, and Edward swept a bow. We all followed suit behind them. I looked up slyly to see how the children did. Jane's curtsey was elegant enough. Harry's bow was enthusiastic rather than dashing. Isabel huffed and puffed loudly in her new stomacher and would have fallen on the ground if Margaret had not caught her.

"Welcome," Edward said. "I hope your journey was bearable."

"Dreadful," said Lady Sherbourne. "We have been jolted to pieces. This is hardly the time of year to be travelling. Three times we got stuck, and –"

"And yet here we are," said her husband smoothly, "arrived safely, before nightfall, and with no real harm done." He stepped forward and grasped his son-in-law's hand warmly, then held his daughter's shoulders to look at her from arm's length. His eyes had the kind gleam they always held for her. He kissed her cheek and she murmured in his ear.

Harry could wait no longer. He bounced forward and put himself directly where his grandfather could see him. He grinned and hopped a little from foot to foot.

"Excellent to see you, Harry," said Lord Sherbourne loudly, offering his hand. "You've grown, for sure."

The boy stood as tall as he could to shake hands, almost raising himself off his heels. "Yes, I have. Mother says I will eat the family out of house and home."

Lord Henry looked down indulgently at Harry. His grey whiskers twitched, but they stopped when another familiar male voice came from the coach. "Greed is a sin, boy. And so is pride."

The excitement that had sparked into fire in my belly was doused with icy water. I sensed Ned edge a little closer to me.

Harry looked at his shoes. I had the urge to step forward and put him behind me, but that was quite impossible. It was Jane, bless her, who reached forward and took her brother's shoulder, pulling him back. Kate and Edward turned to each other, the same question in their eyes.

Edward recovered his composure first. "Ah," he said. "Welcome... cousin." He went forward to shake Father Makepeace's hand as he stepped down. Makepeace looked much as he always had, though perhaps he was even leaner, and his grey gaze more intense. "We thought you were travelling abroad again," Edward said.

"I was," he said. "There was a break in the weather and I was able to get a ship home. God clearly wanted me to be here." He did not smile.

Lady Sherbourne added, "I thank God for that. I was delighted when Mister *Farendon* arrived at our house in time to come with us." Kate and Edward nodded at her emphasis on the name. "Christmas wouldn't be Christmas without... without family."

"*Mister Farendon?*" said Harry in a loud whisper to Jane. "But his name's —"

I leaned forward involuntarily. Kate turned quickly to Harry, but Jane got there before her mother. She squeezed her brother's arm. "Shh!" she said.

"Harry!" his father said quickly. "Take your grandfather into the house and... show him your schoolroom. His last visit was before you began lessons."

Edward looked at Lord Henry apologetically, who nodded curtly and placed a hand on Harry's shoulder. "Lead on, young man," he said. "Let me see where the wonder of your education happens."

Harry's doubtful expression clearly said that he would not have described Master Greene's lessons in those terms himself, but he dutifully led his grandfather inside the house. Lord Henry patted Jane's cheek briefly and took a circuitous route past Isabel, who had begun swaying from side to side in a dangerous manner and attempting a tuneless nursery song, despite mine and Margaret's efforts to make her behave.

Kate let out a sigh and closed her eyes. "No harm done," Edward told her softly. "We are all of us friends here."

Lady Sherbourne tutted. "I'm sure you want to correct the boy very soon, sir," she said, and added more quietly, "There is a good reason why children should speak only when spoken to." She cast an angry look at Isabel, then Margaret and me. Isabel was still jabbering away and making broad gestures with her arms. Margaret made efforts to shush the girl and I tried to hold her hands still. This only made her redouble the volume of her rendition of *London Bridge*. This visit was going very wrong.

"Their foolish talk is dangerous," Lady Sherbourne said, swinging her stare back to Edward.

"Mother, I will speak to Harry about it before supper. He doesn't understand –" Kate began urgently, but her mother cut her off.

"Katherine, it is no longer *your* job to set him right. He is in breeches now. His father must deal with the matter." Lady Sherbourne paused for effect, then said, "and deal with it firmly."

She looked hard into her daughter's eyes. "It is for Harry's good *and* for ours." Kate nodded and lowered her eyes. "You always were soft-hearted, Katherine," her mother said. She turned to Edward. "I am sure your father set *you* on the right path when you spoke out of turn, sir," she said.

Before Edward could respond, Makepeace spoke up from behind Lady Sherbourne's shoulder. "Your mother is right, Lady Spicer. A child who is not corrected is not loved," he said. He was still unsmiling, but I saw the gloating in his stare. My teeth clenched. Edward had always listened to Kate's mother's views and then proceeded to do exactly as he pleased. But Makepeace was a different matter.

Edward bristled at Kate's side and his head twitched upwards from his mother-in-law to Makepeace. His shoulders squared. Even from the back, I knew the hard expression he wore at that moment. I wished I could go to Kate. Her hands were in front of her where I could not see them, but I knew she was moving her wedding ring around on her finger. She had been running Edward's house and raising his children for fifteen years, yet she still feared her mother's criticism.

Edward spoke with an edge. "Of course I will do my duty as Harry's father." He held the other man's gaze into the following silence. My heart sank. I bit my lip. Then Edward asked loudly, to no one in particular, "Shall we go in? The night is coming on fast." He turned on his heel and stalked into the house. His face was tight and his fingers flexed at his sides. He passed close by Ned and tapped him on the arm, and Ned followed him immediately.

Kate watched his retreating back and I managed to catch her eye, willing her to understand my silent support of her. She took a single deep breath. Then she gave her mother a wonky smile. "Come in before you get cold, mother. And Mister Farendon, of course. Molly has put some mulled ale ready."

Lady Sherbourne said nothing, but gave a significant look at Makepeace and one of exasperation at her daughter, which she extended to her namesake granddaughter. Jane dropped into a second curtsey and I followed suit. Her grandmother swept towards the house. I was glad to have been ignored. I came back up just as Makepeace's gaze fell on Kate. She lowered her eyes and gestured timidly that he might walk with her into the house.

Makepeace took the lead from Kate by half a pace, his hands clasped behind his back. "Thank you for your hospitality, Lady Spicer," he said. "Let me assure you that I intend to be of benefit to your family while I am here." It was as well that I was helping Margaret manage Isabel because I could not stop my lip from curling. I must have looked as though I smelt something nasty; Margaret made a questioning face at me.

Kate smiled a tense, nervous smile. He did not return it. He was waiting to judge her answer, as he judged every answer, as he had judged all her answers for years. She might have been a child again, being tested on her *Pater Noster*. "We are grateful to have you with us, sir. God is merciful," she said.

I thought that for a fraction of a moment his eyebrow raised a touch.

"Let us hope so, madam," he said. "There are many in need of it."

CHAPTER THREE

Harry did not escape punishment. He and his grandfather were descending the stairs when Margaret and I brought Isabel back inside, and Ned had come into the hall from Sir Edward's study.

"Your father wants to see you," Ned told Harry, with a pitying look. He nodded over his shoulder at the closed door of Edward's room. Harry looked up imploringly first at me and then at his grandfather. Lord Henry gave the boy a little push towards the door and Harry went with a hangdog expression to knock on it.

"Come," said Edward from behind the door. Harry opened the door gently and slipped inside.

Lord Sherbourne frowned at the door after it had clicked shut. I wondered if he was holding Makepeace responsible for Harry's punishment. Or perhaps he was thinking about supper. Ned and I shared a silent glance. Then Lord Henry shook his head a little and came to himself, nodded at Ned and me, and went to join the others in Kate's parlour.

On our own at last, Ned and I sat on the bottom stair. He took my hand and kissed it, then held it firm in both of his.

"I've hardly seen you today, Moll," he said.

"I know. And the day is nearly over." I yawned, suddenly exhausted. This was the first time I had sat down in hours, and now that I had, I wanted to lie down and sleep. I caught my yawn with the back of my hand and apologised to Ned.

Too late. He began to yawn too, and we both laughed. These moments were precious. One day soon they would not be so rare. One day soon we would be man and wife. In the new year.

"There's a to-do," he said, jerking his head at the closed door of Sir Edward's study. I loved that we didn't need any more words about it. We both knew what was what. I rested my head on Ned's shoulder and closed my eyes.

Soon the door opened and Harry shuffled out, sniffing and wiping his eyes on his sleeve. When he saw us watching from the bottom step, he drew himself more upright and stuck out his little chin.

I offered him my hand, the one that Ned did not have hold of. He walked gingerly but was eager to come and take it. I held his hand and rubbed his fingers with my thumb. It was impossible to say that it wasn't his fault, that Makepeace had made it so that he received a beating. Not only because it wasn't my place; it wasn't fair to confuse the boy.

Harry showed me what he held in his other hand. A bright penny. A beating and a coin in the same minute. Now that was sure to confuse him. I smiled at him, though, and he gave me a watery one in return.

"Papa says that Father Makepeace is only a priest sometimes," he told me, nonplussed.

I couldn't say the right thing for several beats. *Stop and think,*

Molly, before you speak, I heard my mother say. *When in doubt, ask a question.*

"What else does your Papa say?" I asked.

"He says that we have to call him Mister Farendon, like Grandmother's family are called. He's pretending to be just a man, not a priest. But when he wears his priest-clothes and he's saying a service, just for us, then he's a priest again, but when he's wearing normal clothes we have to pretend he's normal like us. Otherwise people will find out he's a priest – people who don't like priests will find out, I mean, and they'll take him away and put him in prison or worse and they might take Father away and Grandfather away and put them in prison or worse too."

That about summed it up. I couldn't have explained it better than Harry just had. And of course, Lady Sherbourne was right. Today's saint might be tomorrow's heretic and none of us could be too cautious. Still, I pitied the boy his beating.

"We must all be careful, then," I said, somewhat redundantly, just for something to say.

Harry nodded. "Papa also said Fath- *Mister Farendon* might have to hide sometimes while he's staying here, if someone comes who might guess *who he really is.*" Harry whispered the last words, cupping his mouth and making his eyes wide. He reminded me of the actors in a stage play we saw when Sir Edward took us to London last year, sharing secrets loudly with the audience. I covered my mouth so I wouldn't laugh. Ned looked away.

The study door opened. Edward emerged with his candle and Ned and I stood hurriedly. Night had fallen while we had been talking and the hall was in near darkness, only a couple of candles lit in the sconces. Edward's face was lit from below.

"I'm sure you can find something that needs doing," he said

to Ned and me. He was an easy-going master, but we knew him in this mood. It was better to be out of his way.

Ned bowed and I bobbed a curtsey, and we hurried away, Ned to help take Lord Sherbourne's luggage from its stowing-place behind the coach, and I to see about linen and a fire for Makepeace's room.

I saw the priest hole of Spicer Hall four times in my life. The first occasion was years ago. After Kate's wedding, we left Sherbourne Manor and came here to live. Edward had just come into his estate. His father had been a clever man, apparently. He made his money in the law and in trade but died before he could finish building, leaving his son with a nearly completed house and master of a fine fortune and a new title while still a young man.

Edward swept Kate from her horse and into his arms to take her across the threshold into her new home. She giggled nervously and clung to his shoulders. It was that rarest of things, a love match.

I hung back, not knowing anyone. The servants seemed just as shy of me. It was Ned that spoke first. I am glad he did or we might all have stood outside all night, waiting for somebody, anybody to lead the way indoors.

"You will think us a rough lot, Mistress Molly," he said. "We have not many women servants, and none so genteel as you."

I stood as tall as I could and inclined my head slightly, determined to live up to his compliments and equally determined to let him know that no nonsense would turn my head.

He let me know by a slight gesture of his hand that I might enter the house at his side. He was the master's manservant. I was the mistress's own maid. I kept a discreet distance between us.

I refreshed myself with a mug of small ale – well-brewed, I was glad to discover – stowed my few belongings in my new room – a bedchamber of my own for the first time in my life, a small but freshly whitewashed room with an adjoining door to Kate's sumptuous new bedroom – then allowed Ned to show me around the house.

It was all so gleaming and new, in the modern style, I supposed, with a particular room for every purpose you could imagine. There was one room dedicated to the sole function of consuming meals. Another room where Edward would go to read and write, with an astonishing number of books – at least twenty, I thought. Ned took a key from its hiding place, unlocked the book cabinet and showed them to me almost as proudly as if he were their owner.

"I am allowed to read them," he told me. "If you don't know how, you'll be expected to learn." I stared like a stupid sheep. "The master says he has no use for servants who cannot read."

I could recognise my name and no more. A little shiver ran through me.

Sherbourne Manor was grand and beautiful, in its old way, with the huge open hall at the centre, and it still felt that I had left my home behind, but Spicer Hall instantly won me over with the smartness that new money could buy. Surely even Lady Sherbourne would be impressed when she came to visit.

While Ned was opening doors for me along a downstairs passageway to let me peek inside, a door behind us flew open. I spun around. Kate stood in the doorway, blushing as only a new bride can.

"Molly, I was coming to call you," she said, beckoning. "In here."

The room was a bright, airy parlour, fitted out for a lady's use. I recognised the fabrics. I had accompanied Kate, before her marriage, to the draper's shop in Rysham and her choices had been sent on. The draper had even closed his shop while we were there. His wife had fussed around Kate, offering her refreshments. Two of the draper's sons fetched and carried patterns and samples. I basked in Kate's enjoyment that day, spending her husband-to-be's money.

Edward leaned casually against the mantelpiece in the parlour. I bobbed a curtsey, nervous of him still, and waited to hear what I was wanted for. He looked over my head. "Ned," he said, "Come in too, and close the door."

I looked behind me at Ned. He came in and pushed the door shut. His reassuring smile made me feel at ease. I wondered what this was all about, all the same. Kate came alongside me and squeezed my arm.

"Show Lady Spicer and Molly where it is, Ned," Edward said.

Ned nodded and went to the panelled wall alongside the fireplace. He tapped along the wooden panels, counting. Then he counted down the mouldings and stopped at one about the height of his knees. He crouched a little, getting a good grip under the moulding with his fingertips. He gave the wood a sudden jerk and stood straight. A section of wainscot the size of a beer barrel clunked loose from the wall and dangled from his fingers.

I understood.

"We aren't likely to need it, of course," Edward said to Kate. "But just in case, you know where it is." He was smiling, rather pleased with himself. He smiled a lot in those early days.

We had a hiding place for priests at Sherbourne Manor, of course. It was an awful little space, just a cramped area behind the false back of a closet. Lord Sherbourne had it made years ago, when King Henry's son, Edward, became king. Those were dangerous days. Then God took him and our Queen Mary brought us back to Rome. That is what my mother told me.

But then she died too – Queen Mary, I mean, not my mother – and none of us knew what the new Queen would do. Perhaps Elizabeth would persecute Catholic priests just as her brother had. One of Elizabeth's new priests took over Makepeace's place in the Church and the parsonage that went with it. I was happy we would have a different man there, though I had grown enough sense to keep that feeling secret. I hadn't grown enough to realise it wouldn't be as simple as that.

Makepeace came to live at the Manor. Kate's parents brought him in to tutor her brother, Robert, as well as to be their own private chaplain – on the quiet. I couldn't feel very sorry for him, especially since I would have to see him all the time. He was brave, I supposed, to refuse to use the new prayers and all that, but I couldn't forget how he had enjoyed Kate's sorrow when Alice died. He wasn't a holy man to me, not any more. I had seen behind that mask – seen that he could do evil deeds just like the rest of us.

So, when Queen Mary died and the Crown went to her sister, that meant I had to clean out the damp, cold space behind the closet in Lord Sherbourne's bedchamber. It was uncomfortable for me in there and I imagined how it would be for him – a tall man – sitting hunched up in the dark. For hours and hours maybe. Maybe there would be rats. I still remember the way the little smile pulled at the corners of my mouth while I scrubbed and swept.

Ned propped the section of panelling he was holding against the wall. Behind was a neat little door slightly smaller than the gap. It had a keyhole with a key but no doorknob. Ned turned the key and the mechanism slid back smoothly. The little door swung outwards with a gentle sigh. He stood back for Kate and me to come forward and take a closer look.

This hiding spot in the parlour of Spicer Hall looked better than Sherbourne Manor's, but not by much. It had been squeezed into the design of the house rather than cobbled together as an afterthought, and I admired the cleverness of it, but I wouldn't want to be shut in.

Stale air flooded from the space behind the door. It would be horribly cramped, not much larger than the one back home. If I sat down inside, there would be not much headroom even for me, and I would have to draw my knees up. I didn't envy any priest having to hide in there. I might not be sorry to see Make-peace uncomfortable one day, but there were other men of God – real ones – too.

I never really thought it would come to that. As far as I could tell from what the family said, this queen seemed happy to let sleeping dogs lie. Nobody would make a fuss about a priest living in a house so long as we didn't make a fuss about some other things.

I knew that Edward did not keep a priest in his house. Kate told me so when she said she wanted me to come with her into her new life. Edward's father had intended to bring a priest into the family and had instructed the builders to make the hole in the parlour wall, but he had not lived to put it to use.

Now that Edward was the master, he had other ideas. While Edward was of our faith, Kate told me, he did not see why we should take unnecessary risks. A visit from a priest now and again was one thing. We would receive the sacraments when we could. But Edward didn't want to be known for keeping one permanently. What if the Queen stopped turning a blind eye, he argued. Kings and queens had been known to change their minds before.

I thought, in the years afterwards, that Edward had been wise to predict how things would turn out. When matters grew worse, and quiet Catholic priests began to be arrested alongside their vocal brothers who hated Elizabeth – or to go abroad as Makepeace often did – it was not Kate and her husband who were watched closely. I thought Kate had done well to fall in love with a sensible man.

After everything, though, I often wonder if this was really how it was. Perhaps it was not wisdom. Perhaps he was led even then by terrible thoughts.

I made up a bedchamber for Makepeace on the east corridor, away from the family rooms. I was glad that the best rooms and newest linen were already in use. Ned brought in his single piece of baggage. He looked around the dingy little room at the cobwebs and raised an eyebrow.

"I had no notice of his coming," I said. "I'll dust it in a minute."

Ned's eyes twinkled at me.

"I'm sure it's good enough for a poor cousin of my Lady Sherbourne," I said. "A *very* poor cousin," I added through gritted teeth.

DEANNE ADAMS

He laughed and soon I laughed too. I couldn't stay angry for long when Ned was around.

Quick light feet sounded on the landing. Jane running again. I hoped her grandmother wasn't close by.

She appeared around the door. Some of her hair had escaped and her cheeks were pink. "Molly, Mother says you can bring in supper now." Jane came close to me and caught my sleeve. I forgot sometimes how big she had grown, tall enough to look me in the eye. Her father would be casting about for a husband for her in just a few years, I supposed. I would soon have to start bobbing a curtsey to her.

She looked earnestly at me, wide-eyed, and spoke low. "But don't bring in the chickens," she said.

I looked at Jane quizzically. I had wrung the necks of the two fattest birds in the yard that morning. Cook had prepared them using her best ingredients. The skin was crisp and brown, and the aroma in the kitchen that afternoon had been wonderful and maddening.

Jane explained. "Father isn't happy about it, I think. But Father Make- ... *Mister Farendon* said that he was sure Mother had ordered a sensible, plain supper because it isn't time for Christmas feasting yet, and he was certain that Uncle Robert and Aunt Ursula would be following the rules of Advent. There are a few days still to wait, he said. And Mother blushed so Father said *of course* – but in that tone of voice, you know – and..."

Her words tailed off. She raised her hands in a shrug. I nodded and managed to stop myself from speaking. Kate wouldn't thank me for using certain words in front of Jane, especially about her brother and that damned wife of his.

She looked relieved that I understood her message and ran

42

back to the family. Ned and I left too, to fetch the family their poor meal of pottage, bread and cheese. I glanced back at the cobwebs in the corners and the dust in the hearth. I clenched my teeth and closed the door on it all. Good enough for him. Very *plain*.

CHAPTER FOUR

The dining room had a good fire so at least there was that comfort despite the lack of meat on the table. Ned and I waited on the family and Makepeace. We sat together in the corner while everyone was eating, despite Makepeace's glare of disapproval. Edward was in no mood to let him dictate how his house was run a third time in one evening, I think.

Harry was subdued. He had only eaten his meals outside the nursery for a few months and proper manners did not yet come naturally to him. I dare say he wanted to avoid a second punishment on the same day. Jane behaved impeccably and answered all her grandmother's questions. Makepeace sat gravely through the meal. He raised the spoon to his lips grudgingly, as if his human needs were abhorrent to him. Lord Sherbourne normally made a meal a lively occasion, but that evening he was irritable. He must have been looking forward to something more satisfying than pottage for his supper.

"The roads were simply dreadful, Katherine," Kate's mother was saying. "Absolutely full of holes. My bones will never be the same again. Fifteen miles we have come in that modern contraption and we went no faster than I could have walked."

"It was you who insisted I buy that coach, madam," Kate's father said. "You wouldn't stop talking about it. Just because Robert bought one for Ursula. It's not my fault you've decided you're too old to ride. When we go home, feel free to walk behind the damned thing, and *I* shall ride."

Edward turned a snort of laughter into a cough. I avoided looking at Ned. Lord Sherbourne drained his mug of beer during the awkward silence that followed and I was glad to have a reason to get up. Edward tapped his mug too and I moved around to fill it. This gave me a good chance to see Kate's face. She was composed, but I knew her too well. Between spoonfuls, she bit her lip and cast glances around the table.

"Molly, top up everyone's beer, will you?" Edward said. "I'll propose a toast."

I included Harry when I got around to the end of the table. Lady Sherbourne's attention fell on him.

"*He* is lucky to be allowed in here at all," Lady Sherbourne said. "If he can't hold his tongue, he should be back in the nursery with Isabel."

I kept my eyes on the jug of beer but sensed that Harry had frozen. Edward broke the silence with a few quiet words. "I think he has been holding his tongue, madam," he said. "He has barely spoken this mealtime."

"Well —" began Lady Sherbourne but stopped. I risked a glance up. The meaning of her husband's look was clear, so she made do with throwing a martyred look in Makepeace's direction. He received her glance impassively, above involving himself in the worldly conversation. Silence fell again.

I stepped back to the corner discreetly and sat down again

next to Ned, the tips of our little fingers touching. Edward raised his mug. The others followed suit, Harry uncertainly, and Make-peace last of all.

Edward declared to the room, "To a journey safely made!" The cheerfulness in his voice was forced but might have passed for genuine to other people. Kate's father raised his mug high in Edward's direction and swigged deeply. Lady Sherbourne dipped her head and sipped. They all drank, except Makepeace, who only touched the cup to his lips.

After the toast, Edward added, "You are welcome here. I hope this Christmas will be the best our family has known." Perhaps it was my imagination – I might be remembering the moment wrongly – but I thought he looked pointedly at Lord and Lady Sherbourne, and not at his third guest. Whether I am right or not, the moment passed, and everyone went back to their food.

There are different types of quiet, I think. Ned and I did not speak in our corner, and not only because we were there to serve. We did not need to speak. The tiny contact of our fingers was enough and our silence was companionable. The quiet at the table was another type of quiet. Our quiet made us happy while theirs oppressed them.

Edward suppressed a smirk. "Ah, Lady Sherbourne," he said, something having apparently just occurred to him. She looked up from her food. "You like to see how your granddaughter's education is progressing, I think."

"Yes, indeed," she replied.

Kate looked nervously at Edward and then at her mother. I was disturbed from my happy thoughts too. This was not a safe conversation.

"Katherine," Lady Sherbourne continued, "let me see Jane's needlework after supper."

Jane looked unable to swallow her food, poor thing. Edward's head was tipped slightly to one side as he always held it when he was amused. I did not see what he found funny. It was Jane who would suffer.

"Yes, of course, Mother," said Kate. She tried to smile. "Jane is practising her sewing by making a shirt – for Harry, of course, not for her father."

Jane winced. Everyone in the house knew how poor Jane was with a needle. Kate had often taught her how to make the stitches small and yet to catch the seam every time. I had also tried and we were very patient. But Jane hardly improved. Every time she attempted this basic stitch, she jabbed at the garment pieces as if she could frighten them into becoming a single piece. Her seams were an inch wide in some places and barely hanging together in others. Hardly surprising, given the way Jane attacked her work as if it were a slippery, deadly enemy.

I do not think she could help it. Jane was clever in many ways, but needlework happened not to be one of them. I watched helplessly as Jane began biting her lip just as Kate sometimes did. Kate had put down her spoon and begun fiddling with her wedding ring. Edward continued to enjoy what he had set in motion. I began to grow angry, partly because I could do nothing about it. Ned took my hand and stroked it with his thumb in just the same rhythm as he would stroke a nervous horse.

Lady Sherbourne approved of Jane's task. She said, "A vital ability for any woman. Easily as important as kitchen affairs. Ursula's girl has a very fine hand with a needle, although she is only ten. I taught you well, Katherine, and I hope you have been teaching Jane the same."

Kate and Jane were obviously uneasy. Edward appeared oblivious to their discomfort. "I was thinking of more serious educational matters than the feminine arts, madam," he said. A little smile played about his mouth. I held my breath. The whole room held its breath. The only sound was the crackle of the fire.

"I see." Lady Sherbourne looked at her husband for support. He had his back to me and I cannot say how he looked. She turned back to Edward. "I am sorry, sir, that you have persisted in this. I am sorry you do not think the *feminine arts* good enough for your daughter. They were good enough for me, and good enough in a wife for you too, when you married Katherine."

Kate and Jane stared at the table. Edward smiled at his wife's mother. I gripped Ned's hand tighter. He had stopped stroking it.

Goaded, as of course Edward had intended, Lady Sherbourne said, "English is enough for any lady to read and write, I think. But Latin? And mathematics too! What is a girl fit for if she is as educated as her brothers? As educated as her *husband?*"

Makepeace set down his spoon. It was the first time he had taken an interest in the conversation. "Do I understand correctly, sir?" he said.

Lady Sherbourne's expression was jubilant at Makepeace's intervention. Edward's smile lost none of its confidence, though. It may have grown wider. "I dare say you do, cousin," Edward said. "You have an excellent understanding."

Makepeace gave the tiniest nod in acknowledgement of the compliment. I felt Ned tense next to me. "A husband is the head of his wife. Her superior," Makepeace said.

"And she is his helpmeet," Edward countered. "How can an

ignorant woman be that?" The smile he wore had lost its amusement.

I prayed he would stop there. Kate's eyes carried the same wish as she looked steadily at him. She managed to catch his eye when he eventually looked away from Makepeace. He seemed to relent, and said, "But of course, Jane is learning the skills to look after a husband too. And music and such-like." He turned his attention back to his food, tearing his bread.

Makepeace watched his host a few seconds longer. His expression was unreadable. Then he picked up his spoon again.

I let out a slow breath. I think Kate did too. She had only agreed to learn Latin and mathematics along with Jane on the understanding that she would do so without people knowing of it. By *people* she especially meant her mother, but she pretended to everyone that she knew no more than any other woman. I understood why. After all, I did not tell people in the village that I had learned to read from Kate – only in English, naturally. It does not do to let everyone know how much you know, not when you are a woman. I was fortunate that some of Edward's ideas had rubbed off on Ned. He loved me anyway.

The family went to Kate's parlour after supper, except Lady Sherbourne, who announced her intention to first visit the nursery. "I must see how Margaret does with Isabel," she said. Although I felt sympathy for Margaret, her absence made the atmosphere in the parlour easier. It might have even been festive had Makepeace not been there, silently forbidding it.

I fetched my sewing from my room and sat in the parlour with the family, as I usually did, to be on hand if they needed anything. From my low stool tucked behind Kate, I had a good view of everyone.

Lord Sherbourne was more of his cheerful self than he had been during supper. I knew why. On my way from fetching my plainwork, I had met him in the hall coming from the direction of the kitchens. He was picking bits of chicken meat from between his teeth with a bone. He grinned at me conspiratorially. I smiled back.

He challenged Edward to a game of chess. I had never understood the game – still don't – but from the way they stroked their beards, each man looked like he might win. Harry watched them play, stroking his own hairless chin. He smiled when his father claimed victory but grew serious again when he realised this meant Makepeace was taking the place of his grandfather to play the winner. Harry edged his stool closer to his father.

As well as my own needlework, I had also fetched Jane's, at Lady Sherbourne's insistence. Her ladyship was determined to make a point. Jane tried her best to produce something decent to show her grandmother when she had finished giving Margaret the benefit of her wisdom and experience. Her cheeks were flushed in the firelight.

Kate showed Jane several times how to make the tiny stitch, very slowly, and talked her through it. Jane nodded and rubbed her eyes. Then she gripped the linen in her left hand and her needle in her right. Her shoulders hunched. She frowned at the two of them and jabbed at the one with the other as if to subdue the garment into being. Kate sighed silently. I wondered how long Lady Sherbourne would be, and whether Kate and I had time to make a few decent stitches on Jane's work for her.

I went into a little fantasy in which Lady Sherbourne came

into the parlour and demanded that Jane bring the half-made shirt to her. She would take the work, peer at it, declare to Jane that she had improved wonderfully, and tell her how proud she was.

I became aware that I was smiling like an idiot when my gaze fell on Makepeace. He observed me coldly. I cast my eyes down at the work in my lap. A moment later I was furious with myself. I was not a little girl any more. I set my jaw and raised my head to look at him again, but he had returned to his chess game.

Kate looked at Jane's work again. I craned my neck to see too. It wasn't a good performance. I hoped Lady Sherbourne had found enough room for improvement in the nursery to take her full attention. Margaret had broader shoulders than Jane.

"You are improving," Kate said to Jane. "This is better than the last one you made." Strictly speaking, I suppose that was true. The two pieces of material were actually joined together.

"Thank you," said Jane, but without a smile. "The last one fell apart the first time Harry wore it," she added ruefully.

Edward looked up from the chess table and laughed. "That's true," he told Kate's father, who was warming his arse by the fire and ignoring his wife's prudish glare.

"Harry wore it when we went riding. We were going along by the river and his sleeve came away with the movement of the horse." Edward ruffled Harry's hair. "D'you remember that?"

Harry grinned. "At least I wasn't in the school room when it happened. I wouldn't like Master Greene to see that."

Lord Sherbourne winked at Harry. "Ah, that wouldn't matter, boy. You would not be the first man to be caused trouble by a woman's mischief," he said. Makepeace nodded, lips pursed, perhaps at the words or perhaps at his plan to win his game of chess.

"Maybe this shirt will last *two* outings," Kate teased Jane. I laughed – to show Jane that it was just a joke.

Jane did not laugh. She rubbed her eyes again. Kate tucked an escaped curl behind Jane's ear. In doing so, she brushed her fingers against Jane's face. Kate's expression became alert and I sat up straight. Kate reached her hand around the back of Jane's neck, feeling the side which did not face the fire.

Kate laid her work on the arm of her chair. I mirrored her action automatically, placing my own work on the table. "Look at me, Jane," she said.

Jane looked up, her eyes bloodshot and circled with shadows. "Are you ill, dear?" Kate asked.

"My head hurts," said Jane. Her voice was strained.

Kate put her hand to Jane's forehead, and then motioned for me to do the same. Jane's blood was raging hot. Kate and I shared a look. We did not need to agree out loud.

"To bed with you," she told Jane. Kate stood up, fetched a fresh candle from the dresser and lit it from the lamp on the sewing table. She put the light in my hand. "Take her up, Molly, and get her down to her shift," she told me. "I'll be along soon."

I took Jane's hand and led her towards the door. Her hand was as hot as her face.

Edward and Lord Sherbourne exchanged concerned glances. Harry looked from one to the other, trying to read their expressions as he had while they were playing chess. Makepeace looked on with mild interest.

Kate followed us out into the hallway. I took Jane upstairs, slowly. She was weak and trembling. Kate disappeared in the direction of the kitchens.

I was tucking Jane into bed when Kate arrived with a bowl of medicine. Jane looked sicker than she had even ten minutes ago. It was not just the dimness of the room creating those shadows on her face. I felt the mattress shift as Kate sat on the edge of it. I fussed about with the sheets until I had arranged my expression into something I hoped was calm and reassuring.

"A good night's sleep will set Miss Jane to rights, to be sure, madam," I said. I could not meet Kate's eyes. I stepped backwards into the darkness away from the bed. Jane had begun shivering.

"Molly's right, dear," Kate told Jane as she leaned over her. "You've caught a chill and you'll feel better in the morning. I have brought some medicine," she said, showing Jane the bowl of crushed sage and vinegar that she'd brought from the kitchens.

Jane wrinkled her nose. "I've added some honey," Kate coaxed. "Come now, we must cool your blood and then you can sleep."

Resigned, Jane opened her mouth and her mother dribbled in some mixture. Jane grimaced but swallowed it. After three spoonfuls Kate passed the bowl to me and pushed Jane's hair back from her face.

"Goodnight, dear," said Kate, and kissed her hot forehead.

"Goodnight, Mother," said Jane weakly, her eyes already closing.

We lifted our candles from the bedside table. In their light, we gazed at her. She looked so much younger than her years. Hard to believe she was thirteen. It seemed only yesterday she was in the nursery.

We left quietly and I closed the door behind us. On the landing, Kate seemed unsure what to tell me to do. "Do you think it's just a bad head, Molly? A chill? Or – do you think it's something more?" she said. Her face was lined with concern.

My gaze went back to the closed door of Jane's chamber.

Jane had been ill before, of course. The usual childhood complaints. But this fever was sudden and violent. "Miss Jane is strong," I said at last. "Try not to worry."

Kate gave an embarrassed smile. "I know I'm overreacting. She'll be better soon. It's just..."

"I understand, madam," I did understand. People were carried off by infection all the time, even the young and strong. I touched Kate's hand for a moment, as she sometimes allowed me to do when she was talking about Alice. "Shall I stay with her?" I said.

"Yes. No. I'll stay with her myself. I don't know if I could sleep anyway," Kate said.

Before I could speak, at the end of the long landing the door opened from the nursery. Candlelight and the voice of Kate's mother spilled out, still advising on child-rearing. Margaret must have had a great deal of advice by now. Kate nodded at me, her decision made. She reopened Jane's door, slipped inside and closed it behind her. I went downstairs before the candlelight could move toward me.

CHAPTER FIVE

The next morning I peeked into Kate's room through the adjoining door. The curtains were open and the night was turning to grey. Kate's bed was still made. I tiptoed along the silent landing to Jane's room.

I opened the door a crack. In the gloom I made out two figures, one tousled in the sheets, the other half hidden in the wing chair, feet resting on a stool. I withdrew and went about the business of the morning.

Cook was kneading the new bread. We nodded our good mornings. I collected my shawl and basket and headed outside to let the chickens out.

It was one of those crisp winter mornings on which the solid ground is spread with patterns of frost. Pretty to look at but dangerous underfoot. I picked my way over the yard, let myself into the enclosure and lifted the henhouse latch. I scattered corn and while they were pecking away, I went into their tiny barn to rummage for eggs.

"Morning, sweetheart," said Ned from the doorway. I

jumped and he chuckled. He could move as silently as an assassin. I made as if to throw an egg at him and he ducked. When I lowered my arm he came close and kissed my cheek.

"Morning," I responded. He put his arms around me and tucked me in close. I put my free hand around his back and rested my head on his chest, listening to his heart. It was a good heart.

Then he spoiled the moment. "Father Makepeace says he will celebrate the Mass and hear confessions in the chapel. Before breakfast." I groaned. "I know," he said, letting me go. "But he's the only priest we've got. Beggars cannot be choosers."

I ended up missing Mass to stay with Jane. When I took my turn at confession later, Makepeace pursed his lips at me although he could say nothing. Lady Sherbourne herself told me to relieve Kate in the sickroom so that she could attend Mass and breakfast.

After my few minutes of peace with Ned, I took fresh ale, medicine and water upstairs and tapped gently at the door.

"Come," answered Kate. Her voice was foggy with sleep. I went in. Kate was standing and stretching. The room was still very dark. A tiny stream of winter sunlight trickled in through the gap at the top of the curtains. A stub of exhausted candle sat on the mantel.

I placed my tray on the table and poured a mug of ale for Kate while she rubbed her fingertips into the back of her neck.

Jane lay tangled in her sheets. One bare leg stuck out of bed and her arms were flung above her head. She must have struggled during the night, but now, in the soft light of morning she could have been a doll, she lay so still.

I bent to examine her. Her cheeks were flushed and her breath was raspy. I placed my hand on the girl's forehead. It felt even hotter than last night. My insides twisted. Her eyelids fluttered open at the touch of my fingers and I forced a smile.

"Good morning, my Janey," said Kate at my side. "How do you feel today?"

Jane did not answer except for a faint whimper. Then she rolled over onto her side and closed her eyes again.

Kate reached around and touched Jane's face gently with the backs of her fingers. Jane groaned at the cold touch and tried to bury herself further in her sheets. Kate looked miserably at me.

"Shall we make her more comfortable, madam?" I asked. "And have a closer look?" I tried to keep my voice light despite my growing fear. Kate nodded and I went to open the curtains for us to see what we needed to see.

Together we peeled the sheets away from Jane. Kate said her name over and over and tried to make her sit up, but she put her arms over her face and rolled away again. The sheets and Jane's shift were sour with sweat. It was slow progress but we coaxed and lifted Jane into a half-sitting position against her pillow. She was weak and a pain somewhere made her reluctant.

Between us, we gently stripped off the sodden shift. I wet a cloth and washed her a little. My eyes moved quickly over her limbs and torso, checking for disease. Kate was doing the same. There was nothing. We breathed our relief in a loud huff at the same time, caught each other's eye and smiled. I fetched a clean shift and we eased Jane into it.

She didn't want to eat or drink – "I feel sick," she said – but we managed to help her take a few sips of small ale and a dose of the medicine. Then we let her burrow back down into her bed and I worked fresh life into the fire.

Kate left to freshen up before going to Makepeace's Mass and I pulled the chair close to Jane's bedside. She was more coherent now she had been moved about, but she was also exhausted by it.

"Do you feel any better?" I asked.

"Not really."

"Oh." I cast about the room for something to do. My eyes fell on a book. Lives of the Saints, I think it was. "Would you like me to read to you?" I said.

"No, Molly. My head hurts."

"Perhaps you should sleep," I said. I stroked her hair as I used to when she was little.

Jane nodded then winced. She closed her eyes. Even with them closed, her eyebrows knotted against the pain in her head. I dipped another cloth in the water, wrung it out and dabbed it on her forehead.

The minutes passed by. The fire crackled. The clock struck nine from the village. Jane's breathing slowed and deepened. The house was quiet. Everyone must have gone to hear Mass in the chapel at the back of the house.

A silent house in the daytime was a strange thing. It could have been that other time, in another quiet house, with Kate ill in bed and everyone but the two of us at church, listening to Makepeace. I watched Jane's face, flushed and tight with fever and pain and it might have been Kate's.

I thought she had drifted into sleep again. It was a surprise when she opened her eyes and spoke.

"Molly," she said, "am I *very* ill?"

"No, dear," I said, maybe too quickly. "Of course not. Everybody catches cold now and again. You'll be up before you know it."

Jane kept her eyes on my face for what felt like an age. I made myself look back. Then she closed her eyes again and her expression smoothed out a little, her brows unknitting. I remembered again that summer day all those years ago and bit my lip.

I remembered not only the silence. I also relived the sourness of the fevered sick chamber masked by the over-sweetness of herbs and flower petals. And yet again, I grew angry when Makepeace delivered to Kate the news that her sister was gone.

Even now, I dreamed of it some nights. His eyes were always shiny black, not grey, and before I woke, I would shout, shout, *"I know you!"* But he escaped through the open window on black wings, his mischief done.

When Alice and Kate were ill, I was sent on errands to fetch this or that all day long. I had been home before to nurse Lizzy, my littlest sister, but I was not entrusted to nurse anyone important. That was left to my mother and to Lady Sherbourne. Their sick chambers held a fascination for me – not of disease, I had seen enough of that – but of Lady Sherbourne when she was not being Lady Sherbourne of Sherbourne Manor, but just herself and a mother. When I came upstairs with whatever I had been sent for, I stood in the girls' doorways before knocking so I could watch her with her daughters. I had only ever seen her schooling and correcting them, or starchily ignoring them in public while they stood back to observe how they should deal with different types of people. Now, in the privacy of the sick chamber, she spoke gently to whichever girl she was with. She stroked Kate's hair. She told Alice she would be well again soon.

The evening before Alice died was a hot and glorious one. Perfect harvest weather. I peeked around the open door to catch another glimpse of the woman behind Lady Sherbourne. Her voice was too low to catch, but I did not need the words. The tone was enough, gentle and murmuring. Her fingertips stroked Alice's cheek.

A footstep behind me made me jump and clutch my bundle of cool linen. Father Makepeace loomed above me. My immediate thought was to be ashamed of spying. My second thought, closely following, was confusion. He was not looking at me but over my head. He was hardly aware of me.

I stepped out of the way. My cheeks reddened and my tongue tried to find a few words, but they died on my lips. Makepeace moved into the space by the door and tilted his head to watch just as I had. A frown made a small crease between his eyes. His mouth opened a little. Had I looked like that?

My reverie fled when the door to Jane's room opened softly. It had to be Kate come to let me get some breakfast. While I had been visiting a time twenty years ago, Jane had slipped into a doze. She was snuffling like a small animal. I chuckled at the noise.

"She's always made that sound when she sleeps, hasn't she, madam?" I said, looking at Jane. "Do you remember when she was tiny? She wouldn't go to sleep in her crib, only against one of us. When she made that noise, we knew we could put her down."

There was no reply and I looked up. Lady Sherbourne stood just inside the door. Her face was ashen. Alarmed, I stood, waiting for instructions. She opened her mouth to speak but shut it again.

I went to her. "What is wrong, my lady?" I asked. Her eyes seemed to implore me. To do what, I did not know. She gestured loosely over her shoulder at the house behind her to explain what she could not say. Dread twisted my gut. I stepped closer.

Had she been Kate, I would have taken her hand. "Who is it?" I asked.

"Harry," Lady Sherbourne said, her voice a whisper. I only heard what she said because she was so close I could feel her breath on my cheek. I couldn't move. I couldn't even think.

"He came with us to Mass," Lady Sherbourne said. "He was quiet. Then at breakfast he sat very still – I just thought he had learned his lesson. Father Makepeace gave thanks and we were all beginning to eat – and then Harry just... crumpled.

"He was so pale. For a moment I thought he..." Her words tailed off. She looked up to meet my gaze. I wondered when she had become smaller than me. Her eyes were wide and frightened. "Your Ned has been sent to fetch the doctor," she said.

I stood rigidly through all of this. It slowly dawned on me that my face must be reflecting Lady Sherbourne's fear back at her.

I moved first. Hesitantly, I touched her hand with the tips of my fingers. She did not scowl or pull away.

"Will you... would you sit with Miss Jane, madam? While I help in the other room?"

Lady Sherbourne sort of woke up then, stepped back, and held herself taller. She spoke with nearly her usual control. "Yes, Molly," she said. "Yes, that is why I came. Go and help."

She sat in the chair I had vacated and fixed all her attention on Jane. I curtseyed and left to see what I could do to help Kate with Harry.

Harry's room was closer to the nursery. I hitched my skirts and trotted along the landing. Both children ill, one so soon after the other. The familiarity of it was horrible. *Isabel.* Was Isabel ill too? The question gave me a fresh stab of fear in my belly. I did not know where I was running to – Harry's room or the nursery.

The decision was made for me. Edward stepped out of Harry's room and I would have run straight into him had he not caught me. His face was taut and his eyes were a little wild. His hands were tight on my arms. I gasped.

"Where have you been, Molly? I was coming to get you –" he said. His words left him suddenly and he released his grip. I shrank away from him. He had never laid a hand upon me before. He was not himself, that much was clear.

I edged around Edward. Harry lay on his bed as limp as a rag doll. Lady Sherbourne said he was pale at breakfast, but he was already feverish. His hair was dark with sweat and stuck to his forehead and neck. He had been stripped to his shirt and it clung to him. Kate stood at his bedside, her hands clutched to her mouth.

"What happened?" I said, more sharply than I meant, but Kate did not notice.

Edward joined us. "He wasn't eating at breakfast," he said. 'Even Kate's father couldn't raise a smile from him. All of a sudden he went white, turned away from the table and vomited. Then he collapsed." Edward motioned helplessly at his prostrate son. "And now... this. He's been opening his eyes, but it's as if he can't see me. He can't talk."

Both Edward and Kate looked at me for answers. For me to take charge.

"Ned has gone for the doctor, yes?" I asked, looking from master to mistress.

They both nodded. I bit my lip. Doctor Phillips lived in Rysham. He would not arrive for hours. Summoning all the confidence I could muster, I said, "He needs to be bled. Can the surgeon be sent for too, sir? Red Will in the village? I am sure Doctor Phillips will advise that."

"Send Old Ned, Edward," Kate said. "Or a stable boy. One of them will be quicker."

Edward shook his head. "I'll go myself," he said. He reached the door in a moment but at it he stopped abruptly. "What about Jane?" he asked me. Something flashed in his eyes – something angry and almost wild again. "Is she like this?" He gestured to the bed.

"No, sir," I said. "I would have told you. *We* would have told you." My heart seemed to pop up into my throat. I moved closer to Kate.

I was glad when Kate spoke up. "No, not like this, Edward." Her voice tremored a little. His glare left me and fixed on Kate. "She is not well, but it is a chill, surely? They've both caught a chill."

I looked at my hands. A few minutes ago I would have reassured Kate that Jane certainly had a chill from being out in the cold. I would have told her that, yes, of course Jane would soon recover. I would probably never have had to tell her how dangerous the signs appeared to be and how worried I was. But now, for both children to be so unwell... I was beginning to feel it would be a lie.

I kept my head bowed until Edward's quick steps sounded on the landing. When I looked up, Kate caught my hand and held my gaze. "What could it be, Molly?"

"Many things, madam," I said. There was no more honest answer.

Kate persisted. "What do you think it is?"

"Too early to tell," I said stubbornly. "We must wait for the doctor." I knew what the next question would be. Desperately, I said, "Let me fetch some things to cool Harry with, madam. I won't be long." I fairly raced onto the landing before Kate could make me stay.

I returned from the kitchens with cool water, linen cloths and medicine. Thankfully, Cook had not long made up a fresh supply. To reach Harry's room I had to pass Jane's. The door was not quite shut. I only meant to check all was well and then be on my way.

But I heard Lady Sherbourne's voice crooning to Jane in that soft way I had last heard twenty years ago. I could not help myself. I might have been a child again at Alice or Kate's door.

"I know, I know," she was saying over and over. "It will all be well."

I shouldn't have looked. Lady Sherbourne was stroking Jane's hair. The tears welled in my eyes and my mouth went trembly. I started when Lord Sherbourne spoke. His voice came from somewhere near the window.

"Jane," he said, and I knew he meant his wife not his grand-child. He sounded breathless like someone who was crying. "Before. Was it like this?"

Lady Sherbourne turned her head slightly, away from me, thank goodness, to speak over her shoulder. "Yes," she said. "It was just like this."

CHAPTER SIX

Shortly after the clock struck three, Ned returned from Rysham with Doctor Phillips. I ran to open the door. The weather had turned. I caught a brief sight of Ned, his hat pulled down and his collar up, before he trudged away to the stables with the sweating horses.

The doctor came into the house, dripping muddy water on the stone floor. He had become portly in his middle age and was puffing after his ride from town. He handed me his travelling bag and removed his cloak and hat. I took those as well.

"Molly, sir," I said.

Doctor Phillips looked more closely at me. Recognition appeared on his face. "Ah, yes," he said. "Good. A sensible servant in the house."

I swelled with pride and volunteered the children's symptoms and everything we had done. I hesitated to tell him that the surgeon was already in the house and had seen the patients, but he nodded in approval.

Edward came into the hall from the direction of the chapel.

He looked unkempt, quite out of character. He strode up to the doctor and I stepped back discreetly.

"Sir Edward," said Phillips, and bowed. His manners, as ever, were impeccable. The only sign he gave that he had noticed the strain on Edward was the soothing tone of his voice. It was the same tone I had heard Ned use to calm a horse.

"If I might put on my gown and mask," he said, gesturing to the travelling bag in my hands, "and visit the patients?" The wild look came into Edward's eyes again, and I flinched. Phillips added quickly, "Purely a precaution against sickness in the air. Whatever it might be. Many illnesses spread themselves through smells. I always wear them until I know what I am dealing with."

Phillips waited. Sir Edward closed his eyes and pinched the bridge of his nose. Phillips waited some more. His expression was calm and even. I felt quite in awe of him.

Edward took a long breath to compose himself before he opened his eyes. He drew himself upright. "Yes, of course," he said. He blinked at Phillips, as if seeing him properly for the first time since he arrived. "You are married, I think, Doctor?" he said. "You have children?"

"Yes, sir."

"Then perhaps you understand." He seemed to want to say more but settled for saying, "You must forgive me."

Edward did not wait for Phillips' response. "Take the doctor to my study," he told me. "Then bring him upstairs."

He turned on his heel and headed for the staircase himself. Again, his face had taken on that demented expression. Cook herself had come from the kitchen with ale for the doctor – it was all hands on deck with two sick children to care for – and she stepped back hurriedly to keep out of his path. Edward did not seem to see her. He took the steps two at a time as if pursued by a devil. I bit down on my lip.

I cast a sideways glance at Doctor Phillips as he watched Sir Edward go. His face was thoughtful. I supposed not every father reacted this way to a child's illness. I offered him the ale that Cook had brought. He took a long swig and then I showed him into the study.

He opened his travelling bag and brought out a long, waxed coat made of thin leather. I helped him into it.

"You definitely have seen no buboes, Molly?" he asked. The door was closed, yet he said this quietly, confidentially.

"No, sir."

"And no lesions?"

I paused. He looked at me sharply.

"Not yet," I said. "I expect to find them every time I look." The words tumbled out. This was the first time I had spoken my fear out loud. I had not even voiced my worry to Kate – in fact, least of all to Kate.

He pursed his lips. Professional concern passed across his face, followed by something else, another thought entirely. "I understand Lord and Lady Sherbourne are visiting," he said.

I said that they were.

"Any other visitors to the house, Molly?" he asked. He asked it so casually I was almost wrong-footed, fool that I was.

Doctor Phillips fixed his eyes on me. The blood rushed to my face and I could not hold his gaze. He knew the family well. He had served them for many years, as far back as Kate and Alice's childhoods. He would perhaps remember Makepeace. After far too long a pause, I said, "A cousin of my Lady Sherbourne, sir. Mister Farendon."

"Indeed," he said. The word hovered between a question and connivance.

I swallowed hard and made myself look him in the eye. I could have kicked myself for not asking Lord Sherbourne what to tell the doctor. *Say no more,* I told myself. Silence is no evidence. And I had perhaps said enough already.

The moment hung in the air. Eventually, it passed. Doctor Phillips picked up his beaked mask and wide-brimmed hat from the table, and said, "Let's see what's wrong with those children, shall we?" He led the way back into the hall and up the stairs. I followed, cursing my own stupidity.

Doctor Phillips examined Jane first. I knocked on the door. It was several seconds before Edward's voice said, "Come."

Edward and Kate were standing ready to receive the doctor. Her cheeks were not currently wet but her mouth was slippery and red blotches mottled her face. Edward had aged within a day. He was colourless but it was more than that. He had a haunted look. I imagined what my knock at the door had interrupted: them clinging to each other, clutching each other like two drowning souls.

I stared at the floorboards as I announced the doctor. He had put on his hat and his contagion mask. The mask was the near white of old bone. The eye sockets were deep and the brim of the hat made them darker still. The bird-man bowed.

His voice was warm, though, when he said, "Lady Spicer."

He drew himself upright and inclined his beak towards the bed where Jane lay asleep. Kate stepped back a pace, silently giving him permission to approach.

I went with him and peeled back the sheets. Kate and I had

changed her shift a second time that day and her sheets too, but the sour smell of sickness was ripe in the air. The movement roused her from her sleep and she opened her eyes. They became like saucers when they latched on to the doctor at her bedside. She grasped at the sheets and tried to pull them back up to hide beneath them.

He tried his best not to frighten her. "I'm the doctor. I'm here to help," he said.

She looked at me, her eyes still enormous. I nodded and smiled to encourage her. Doctor Phillips did not move. He waited for her to decide for herself. She gradually eased her grip on the sheets.

"Thank you, Miss Jane," he said.

By this time, Jane's condition was more alarming. She had begun to suffer pain all over. She complained of it when she was awake and it was written on her face when she was sleeping. Her eyes had sunk into her face, surrounded by dark circles. Doctor Phillips took his time examining her and studying the blood taken by the surgeon, and he ordered that her water should be collected too.

I showed Doctor Phillips from Jane's room to Harry's, my heart in my mouth. Lady Sherbourne stood to make room at the bedside. She acknowledged the doctor's presence with a slight nod, then went to look out the window into the darkness.

Harry's condition had become frightening. He was raging hot and slipping in and out of delirium. While in these episodes, he shouted terrified nonsense and thrashed about as though possessed by a demon. It was as well that Kate and Lady Sherbourne had decided that the three of us would manage the children between us. The ignorant girls' wagging tongues would set gossip running through the village like the plague.

Harry was in one of his vacant, quiet phases and there was no resistance at all, not even recognition that a stranger in a mask was in his room. I wondered what reaction the doctor wore behind his mask.

The doctor poured Harry's blood from the shallow bowl in which it had been collected into one of his flasks, stoppered it, and swirled it around, just as he had with Jane's. He was observing the humours, that much I knew. I was fascinated by the darkness of the liquid and the way it clung to the inside of the glass. I wondered what the doctor could tell from it.

After the examination, Doctor Phillips asked in a low voice, muffled through his mask, to speak again with Edward and Kate. I expected Lady Sherbourne to speak. I thought she would instruct me to remain with Harry so she could go along and hear the diagnosis. Instead, she returned to the bedside and sat down again, watching Harry's face. Her silence forbade me to speak either. Nor did she respond to the doctor when he bowed. We left the room awkwardly and I closed the door. I thought I heard a sob.

Doctor Phillips removed the hat and mask and passed them to me. I took them without a word. Anything I could say about Lady Sherbourne would have been beyond my position. Feeling embarrassed and nervous, I took the doctor back along to Jane's room and knocked on the door, expecting to wait for an answer again.

Edward flung open the door and I jumped back. He looked eager and terrified in equal measure. Kate joined him at his elbow the next moment. I looked to Doctor Phillips.

"May I speak with you and your wife, sir?" the doctor said.

They came out onto the landing. Kate caught my arm to stop me from taking her place at Jane's side. "I need you to know what is wrong too, Molly. You may as well hear it from the doctor."

Kate's voice tremored. Mine would have done too if I had spoken. I stood back and waited for the doctor to speak.

Doctor Phillips said, "It is not certain how this fever will manifest itself. It may simply break. As for the cause, both children have an excess of blood, particularly your son. You must send again in the morning for the surgeon –" indicating the dark liquid that had settled in the flasks "– for both children."

Edward and Kate nodded. Behind them, I nodded too, relieved I had done the right thing in asking for Red Will to come today.

The doctor still looked serious. "However," he continued, lowering his voice further, "the symptoms are those I would expect of smallpox. And there have been cases in the county, some of which I have seen myself. You must prepare yourselves for that."

Kate gasped and covered her mouth with her hand. She half-turned towards Edward and clutched at his sleeve. He turned his head toward the door and put his hand against the doorframe, supporting himself. I held my breath.

Doctor Phillips waited for them to gather themselves. "Do not lose hope," he said. "Continue to care for them as you have been. They are in danger, yes, but your care is excellent. I will attend them again in the morning. Beyond that, their recovery is in the hands of God."

Edward did not respond. When she saw that he was not going to speak, Kate said, "Yes. Yes, it is in God's hands. We all pray that He spares them – don't we, Edward?"

She only glanced at Edward. Her attention was on the doctor. But I watched Edward. While he nodded along to Kate's words, a flush grew upwards from his collar. He rubbed his hands together and stared at them.

I narrowed my eyes. In all the years I had been in his household, I had only seen him behave like that once before. On that occasion, he had had something to be ashamed of.

We all knew about it, all of us who worked there. Kate was in confinement, expecting Isabel any day. Ellen, a maid from a decent family in the village, simpered around the house, the lovestruck little idiot. At first, I thought she'd taken up with one of the menservants, perhaps even Ned. So I watched her carefully and soon I noticed that whenever Edward passed by she blushed and grew tongue-tied.

If it had been a one-sided infatuation, I would have boxed her ears for her stupidity and told her to put her mind to her work. But Edward had a soft spot for her. He chucked her under the chin when she brought his dinner, that sort of thing. She soon let her vanity get the better of her. She disappeared for an hour most days and reappeared wearing a soppy little smile. Fool.

I didn't tell Kate. There was no point in upsetting her, or that's what I told myself. It might harm the baby she was carrying. It was natural for a man, especially when his wife was unable to join him in his bed. More of a surprise that this was the first time. I told myself those things too.

I should have told Kate. It might have softened the blow for her.

I was cleaning the baby while she rested in bed. Edward was visiting them. Kate asked Edward, "What is happening in the outside world?"

"Nothing of consequence," he said, his eyes fixed on his hands. He rubbed intently at an invisible smudge of dirt on one thumb. The colour rose upwards from his collar.

When he left the room, it did not take Kate long to get the truth out of me. I'll never forget how she looked.

The affair was over soon enough. Kate healed and got her strength back. Edward was all loving attentiveness to Kate once more and she packed Ellen off, back to her family, and that was that. I don't know how else the girl could have expected it to end.

And now, that way in which he rubbed his hands together, concentrating on them to the exclusion of all else. The redness creeping up his neck into his face. He was concealing something, of that I was certain.

I left Kate and Edward at Jane's door and showed Doctor Phillips to his own hurriedly made-up bedchamber. The new concern I felt for Kate that Edward had a secret, one he was keen to *keep* secret, played on my mind. Not in my wildest thoughts could I have hit upon what it was.

CHAPTER SEVEN

Doctor Phillips and I were right. More's the pity. The following day, pox lesions erupted first in Jane's mouth and, within hours, on her face. The day after that, they ravaged her arms and legs. They spread as we watched.

From the moment we saw the first fluid-filled pustule rise on Jane's skin, the misery in the house heightened into terror. When the rash broke out on Harry's skin too, we collapsed into numbness and despair. The only saving grace was Isabel's stubborn good health. I did my best to hide from Kate the horror I felt and threw myself into my work.

Not that I had to find excuses to be busy. Extra hands could not be found in the village, not once the word was out that the house had sickness in it. All of us women were busy. I was everywhere at once, it felt. I fetched and carried, served meals wherever the family happened to be, prepared the medicines and emetics Doctor Phillips ordered, nursed the children, stripped their soiled sheets, and when I wasn't doing all of that, I was on my knees in the chapel with anyone else who was available. Ned was occasionally there at the same time. A smile, a squeeze of the hand, and a few words were all we could share in those days. I took snatches of sleep where and when I could. Aches stiffened my shoulders and my eyelids drooped with exhaustion.

Edward came to the chapel often, though he stared vacantly more often than he prayed. Kate came too, although she could hardly bear to be away from the children. Lord Sherbourne spent hours there, his head bowed. Lady Sherbourne was the most silent I had heard her in years.

Makepeace was there all the time, or so it seemed, admonishing us repeatedly to repent of anything and everything we could remember. I made confession, telling him of my prideful-ness and recent unkind thoughts. He fixed me with his steady grey gaze when I was done.

"Anything else?"

I met his eyes. "No, Father," I said. "I have not stolen apples in years."

I hid my insolence behind a neutral expression with diffi-culty. He paused, reluctantly moved to the absolution, and then let me go. I felt his eyes on my back.

Doctor Phillips came to the chapel too, heard Mass and made confession along with everyone else. Ned served at supper the first evening the doctor spent with us, and later, during one of our snatched moments together he whispered that Lord Sher-bourne had introduced the doctor and Mister Farendon, as if the one had not just confessed his sins to the other.

So, for the whole of his stay with us, in any other part of the house Doctor Phillips talked on an equal footing with Mister Farendon, while in the chapel he deferred to the same person as a priest. Another time I would have laughed at the nonsense of it. It was just like one of those London plays where everyone is really somebody else.

It was not that nobody cared any more that Makepeace should remain *incognito*. It was more that there was never a greater need to reach out to the Almighty, and for that we needed Makepeace. Besides, it became as though Doctor Phillips was part of the household, bound to us in our common struggle against the disease. To put it simply, we trusted him.

Red Will, the surgeon, came out from the village twice a day. It often fell to me to hold the bleeding bowl while he worked. I couldn't have done Will's job. My stomach is strong enough with regards to blood and so on, but all that setting of bones – it's enough to make me shudder. Ned told me once how one of the farm labourers screamed and swore fit to scare the Devil away when Red Will pulled on his arm. He was a decent enough fellow to have in the house, though. He had better manners than most working men, and he was gentle and quick as could be with the children.

Poor Harry. He suffered badly for four days. He thrashed about and burned up, fighting all the way. On the fifth day, shortly after dawn, his fever seemed to break and he became lucid.

Our relief was short-lived, however. As the morning ground on, on the day which for the rest of the world was St Stephen's Day, Harry grew colder and colder, and ever weaker. His lips turned blue and his skin became grey. We added more and more blankets and kept the fire roaring, but nothing helped. Nothing could hold his interest, not even his grandfather who came in to make him laugh.

That afternoon, his breathing became laboured, his belly rising and falling rapidly. I was with him when the church clock struck four and I had to light a candle. I observed that he had slipped into a deep sleep. I ran out on the landing and called for Doctor Phillips, though I knew that neither he nor anybody else could rouse him. In honesty, I did not want to be with him alone. That midwinter evening, Harry died.

Kate sat by the bed and rubbed Harry's limp hand as if she would chafe life back into him. His nose and cheekbones were sharp, and his cheeks were waxy in the candlelight. I touched Kate's arm but she shook me off roughly. She rocked herself backwards and forwards, her breath coming in gasps, and unaware, I think, of the wetness of her face. I had been holding back my own tears for days and now they flooded out. They streamed out of me and my nose ran while I waited for Kate to be ready for me to touch her. Edward sat apart, close to the window, a statue with his head in his hands.

Makepeace had blessed a phial of oil so that Harry would not pass without being anointed. He finished speaking the Latin over Harry's body and stoppered the phial. His face was grave but his eyes were entirely dry. He put his head on one side, just slightly, observing Kate. And for the second time, though twenty years apart, I watched him watching her and saw his eagerness, how he revelled in her pain. How he fed off it, as a raven feeds off a cadaver.

He placed his hand on Kate's shoulder. "Let us pray the sin which brought him death will not keep him long from his place in Heaven," he said, looking down his long nose at her. She nodded speechlessly, her face almost as still and pale as Harry's. Her eyes gazed ahead, unseeing. But I saw the perverse gleam of pleasure in his eye. It was through a red mist, but I saw and I longed to claw his eyes out for it.

A muffled cry, a raw noise of pain rose from behind me. At

first, I did not know it and I spun around at the new threat. Edward was looking up from his hands, hurt flooding his eyes. The animal sound broke through Kate's numb fog of grief for the first time since Harry stopped breathing. I felt her get to her feet behind me and her hand grasped for mine.

Makepeace stepped backwards towards the door, his hungry look gone now that he was faced with something wilder than himself.

My eyes flicked across to Edward. He was barely recognisable in his white-hot rage. He bared his teeth at the priest. Makepeace took another involuntary step backwards.

Edward stood and his chair toppled and crashed on the floor. In that moment, he seemed a giant to me. I turned to Harry, afraid the noise would wake him, would frighten him, and then I remembered. A fresh stab of grief cut through me, mixed with a rush of blood in my ears. This was not the husband of my mistress, my Kate. I pulled her backwards out of the path between the two men.

"Is *that* your comfort?" shouted Edward, jabbing a finger at the priest. His jaw jutted. Spittle flew from his mouth. "I have lost my *son!*" He came towards Makepeace, now rooted to the spot. He came right up close, toe to toe, staring down into his face.

Makepeace fell back half a pace and seemed to shrink, the colour draining from his face. His hands came up to ward off his attacker and his mouth fell open, flapping silently.

"He is dead." Edward almost spat the words, speaking lower now, but more threateningly. "What do you think *you* can say? What do *you* know about it? What good did your prayers do? *Nothing!*"

Makepeace stammered out a few words. "It must be for the

best," he said. "The best thing for the boy's soul. God –" but he got no further.

Edward grabbed the man by the shirt. His knuckles were as tight as his face, though they were white and his face was flushed. "What are you saying? He deserved to die? He was wicked and he *deserved* to *die*?" Makepeace grew even paler. They both shook. Edward's fingers twisted in Makepeace's clothing to keep him close, though he didn't seem capable of pulling away.

"You come here into *my* house... you come uninvited... you put my family in danger... and you tell me my son is better off dead?"

This was the first time I had seen Makepeace lost for words. I was too shocked to enjoy the moment. The next few moments would have soured my pleasure anyway.

Kate and I clung to each other. She found the use of her legs before I did, let me go and hurried towards Edward. I stretched an arm after her, my mouth open, yet no words would come. She pulled at his arm, trying to loosen his hold on the priest. "Edward, stop!" she cried. "Stop! You mustn't."

But her husband was beyond listening. It wasn't even him any more. He was possessed. He let go of Makepeace's shirt with the hand she was pulling at and shoved her. Hard. She fell heavily to the floor. My legs still wouldn't move.

The next few seconds took forever. Fast footsteps sounded on the landing. The door flew open and Doctor Phillips and Ned appeared in the doorway. Seeing Ned, my body unfroze itself. I ran to Kate, knelt down and put an arm around her. She was silent but her eyes filled with shock and grief. I cradled her against me.

Doctor Phillips assessed the situation. He stepped slowly

into the room. He held his hands out in front of him, priestlike, welcoming the flock into the fold. He halted a yard short of the two men and planted his feet firmly, setting himself where Edward could see him. Ned followed him quietly into the room but hung back.

"Sir Edward," said the doctor. His voice was hardly more than a murmur, yet it commanded. Everyone turned to look at him, including Edward, who still had hold of Makepeace's shirt. Even Makepeace took his eyes off Edward's face and swivelled them towards Doctor Phillips.

"You need to let him go," said the doctor.

Edward looked past Makepeace at his son. The humanity slowly returned to his eyes. It seeped outwards to his face, which softened and then crumbled. His fingers loosened their grip and his shoulders slumped. Makepeace disentangled himself and stepped backwards towards the door. He was pale and shaken. At the door, he stopped, unsure whether to go or stay. Something new came into his face as he looked back at Edward, something that fought with his fear. I thought at first it was anger. I expected a flash of anger. But it was not. It was a gaze of calculated hatred and it chilled me to the core.

Makepeace stayed long enough to see Edward's knees give way, then turned on his heel and left. A small pink patch had appeared on each of his cheeks.

Ned started towards Edward but was stopped by Doctor Phillips' hand on his shoulder. He directed Ned towards Kate and me instead. Ned silently offered Kate his hand and helped her off the floor. She composed herself, breathing deeply. I stood by and smiled at Ned in a way I hoped was reassuring. He squeezed my hand briefly.

Kate nodded at Phillips in thanks, who bowed and left the

room. Ned tugged my hand. I did not move. Then Kate gave me a small nod too.

I was reluctant to leave her, but Kate had already turned her attention to her husband, on his knees, bowed and exhausted. We crept out and closed the door behind us, leaving Kate with her broken husband and her dead son.

I stayed with Jane that night, in the truckle bed at the end of hers. I slept, once I had cried myself out, and woke in the grey light of morning to find her cool and breathing peacefully in her sleep. I could have laughed aloud if it were not for Harry. The midwife would come later this morning to wash Harry, and then we would take him to the churchyard.

Jane stirred gently and I made my best effort not to wake her. Sleep was the best medicine. Besides, she would discover soon enough that she had lost her brother. Let her have a little more time not knowing, I thought.

I crept out of Jane's room. Lady Sherbourne was at the top of the stairs, about to descend. I bobbed a curtsey and came up with a broad smile and a gesture back to Jane's door. She placed a hand to her mouth and sobbed but I knew she too was smiling through it. Her eyes glistened and crinkled in just that sort of way. I grinned back.

I could not wait for Doctor Phillips to confirm it. I had to tell Kate the good news. I went immediately to her bed and roused her, averting my eyes from the figure of her husband beside her.

She opened her eyes slowly at first, then became instantly alert. "What?" she said. "Jane?" She flung back the covers. Edward moved too.

I spoke quickly to reassure her. "I think she will live, madam," I said. I could not hide my broad smile nor disguise my tears. "I believe she will live."

Breakfast was a peculiar affair, a daily event in the most bizarre of circumstances. Bread was broken, and then a child would be buried.

Jane had woken briefly, drunk some small ale and gone back to sleep. Doctor Phillips announced she was out of danger and could be safely left alone for a time so I waited on the family, plus the doctor and Makepeace. Yet at that moment Harry was being tended to by the midwife who had delivered him into the world seven years ago. I had seen her work both with the newly born and with the newly dead and I could picture the tasks she and her assistant were carrying out.

The tears welled up again and my chin wobbled. I wondered if anyone else's thoughts were travelling along the exact path as mine. Lady Sherbourne sat very upright. She barely touched her morning bread. A stranger – and not just a stranger but most people who thought they knew her – would have thought her cold, yet I knew there was turbulence beneath her self-control.

Lord Sherbourne made brave but doomed attempts at conversation once or twice. Not even he could raise the mood. The doctor politely answered queries about his family but did not volunteer more information. For the first time it occurred to me that he was missing out on the festivities of Christmas. He looked at his breakfast with disappointment, or I felt he did, at any rate. No wonder he had mentioned returning home today. I determined to find him something tasty from the kitchen before he left.

Makepeace ate his breakfast in the manner he always did, as though feeding his body gave him no pleasure. The events of yesterday had had no effect on him. Neither grief nor embarrassment appeared to touch him. He looked about him with the same cool grey gaze, as though nothing was amiss. I didn't know why, not at the time, but this troubled me more than any look of resentment would have done.

I believed I knew Kate's and Edward's thoughts. Much the same as my own, I imagined. Neither ate. Edward stared at the ceiling. Kate was pale, naturally, and her eyes were reddened. She fiddled constantly with her wedding ring. She also had the little crease between her eyes that she got when she was thinking.

When I had cleared away the breakfast and managed to swallow a few mouthfuls myself in the kitchen, I went to Kate's room to help her prepare for church. She was waiting for me in her chair. It was obvious which gown she would require – the precious black silk – and I went to the closet to fetch it.

I unwrapped the dress on the bed, the lavender fragrance billowing from the linen, and shook it out ready for Kate to put on. I was determined to only think of the job I had to do. Tears now would mark the silk.

Kate stood and put her back to me so I could unlace her everyday gown. She looked over her shoulder while I unknotted the cord.

"Molly."

"Yes, madam?" I said, eyes on what I was doing.

"Molly – do you remember when I was ill?" she said.

There was no need to ask which illness she meant; only one mattered. My fingers froze for a sliver of a moment. She turned her shoulders to see me more directly.

"Of course," I said.

"And you remember what happened. You know, when I began to recover. Who told me... when I found out that Alice was gone."

It was not a question. Makepeace, eager and raven-like. *Pray for your own salvation.* I stalled for time, helping Kate to step out of her skirts.

"I did not know you remembered that, madam." I bit my lip and turned to the bed, putting the woollen gown aside. Stupid thing to say. Of course she remembered.

I turned back with the black silk and she was facing me. Her eyes were knowing. I felt my face go red and I looked away.

"I want you to stay home, Molly," she said.

I looked back at her, startled, then open-mouthed. Not come with them to bury Harry? Hadn't I cared for him since his birth? Hadn't I done as much as Kate to raise him? I pooled the gown at her feet for her to step into.

The silence was thick as pudding while I shimmied the gown over the petticoats. I wasn't family, I knew that. Naturally, I wasn't needed. We stood in silence while I laced up the dress.

My face must have been quite mulish when I was done, because Kate came close, paused a moment, then put her arms around me for the first time since we were girls. I was too surprised to react – and too sullen, if I'm truthful.

"I know Father Makepeace speaks truth about God's will, Molly. I do not deny that," she murmured in my ear. "But I would not wish Jane to hear about her brother as I heard about Alice. Stay with her while we are at church. If she wakes and must be told, *you* tell her. Understand?"

I put my arms around Kate too. The tears sprang out again. Drat. The silk. I pulled away and dabbed at the mess I had made on her shoulder. She gave a half-smile, we both dried our faces, and then we finished dressing her to take her child to the churchyard.

Reverend Smyth, one of the new churchmen, arrived to lead the funeral party. He waited in dignified silence. Makepeace stayed out of sight in the chapel. The parson and he had met several times over the years, before total secrecy was necessary. Each meeting had been uncomfortable. A meeting now would be a disaster.

Every pair of eyes looked as four of our men bore the coffin downstairs. Ned was in front, his face stony. At his side was Ned's father. His jaw was clenched and his nostrils flared. Old Ned passed close by me when they manoeuvred into their place in the procession. I saw his eyes were wet.

Kate leaned lightly on Edward's arm, who seemed to be present in body only. The whole village would know by now that one of the children had been taken. The route would be lined despite the Christmas season. I watched Kate take Harry to church for the last time and I knew that not one of those people would be able to say that Lady Kate Spicer trembled.

CHAPTER EIGHT

As it happened, Jane did not wake for hours. I heard occasional stealthy footsteps pause outside the room, but they moved away again. I knew it was not Margaret with Isabel. Isabel did not go anywhere stealthily. I imagined Makepeace straining to hear our voices and I triumphed that he was denied the chance to interrupt.

The house slept too. It seemed to be resting, taking time to heal from the hurt of the past week, just as we all needed to. I sat at Jane's bedside with some knitting, soothing myself with the rhythm and click of the needles. It was going to be a hat for Ned. I smiled to know that soon I would have a husband to look after. He had waited a good long time for me to agree to marry him and now it was I who was impatient. A few more weeks to wait, that was all.

The house woke again gently. A few servants had been sent ahead to stir up fires and prepare refreshments, no doubt. Doors opened and closed downstairs. Voices murmured. Then the activity became urgent. The front door closed with a bang. Boots clattered across the stone flags of the hall, disappeared somewhere into the house, and came back again half a minute later, running elsewhere.

I put my knitting to one side and went to the door to peek out. Everything was calm again. I closed Jane's door behind me, moved to the head of the stairs, and saw the top of Ned's head in the hall. He was coming from the direction of Kate's parlour.

"Ned?" I called in a loud whisper.

He jumped visibly and spun to look up the stairs. He puffed out a sigh of relief when he saw it was me and gestured for me to come down to him.

I came as far as the bottom step so I could look him in the eye. He was flushed and breathing hard.

"What's wrong?"

"Had to put the Father... in the hole," he said in an undertone.

It took me a moment to digest this. When I had, my mouth fell open and I looked instinctively towards the passageway that led to Kate's parlour.

Still breathless, Ned explained that Reverend Smyth was returning with the family. I was puzzled and my face told him so.

"Sir Edward has invited him back. Said he was moved by the service he gave for Harry and would he come back and see all over the house and then sit and talk with him –"

"What for?" I said.

It made no sense. Edward and Kate kept Smyth at arm's length. He was one of the new sort, the ones the Queen wanted us to have. When Edward accepted him for the position, Kate told me the type he was. She wasn't happy to have a Lutheran there but she could see that it was sensible to not make a fuss.

Better to conform in public, attend services, and do our own thing quietly.

That was years ago. He turned out to be a decent man, despite being made of the wrong cloth. He made himself busy with the welfare of the villagers, I gathered, and rarely ventured up here, except when there was urgent business with Edward that could not wait until Sunday.

And now he was coming to see the house at Edward's invitation. While Makepeace was here.

Oh.

Ned watched my face and nodded along while I went through these stages of thought and ended up at the truth.

"Everyone heard Sir Edward invite Smyth – Lady Spicer, her parents, everyone. You could have cut the air with a knife. Lord Sherbourne sent me ahead to give the Father five minutes' warning. Yes –" Ned said, seeing I was about to exclaim how much trouble this would cause, "– he knows exactly what he's done. He seems to be looking forward to it."

Ned shrugged his shoulders yet looked worried. "Nothing we can do about it, Moll. Let's hope he doesn't stay long."

My hand flew up to my face. "Ned!" I said. "I haven't cleaned it! I was going to but then the children got ill. It went out of my head. It's not been opened in years."

But there was nothing to be done. The door opened, letting an icy blast into the hall. Lord and Lady Sherbourne came through first, faces as cold as the weather. Then came Edward with Kate on his arm. Reverend Smyth followed, looking pleased with himself and with his invitation. Kate still wore her thick veil but I could tell she was agitated from the way she grasped her cloak. She let go of Edward's arm as soon as they were in the house and stepped quickly across the flagstones towards me, unpinning her veil as she went.

I helped her remove the pins. Kate looked at Ned, silently demanding to know if Makepeace had been hidden. Ned bowed his head as a yes and I touched her hand ever so slightly, knowing she would understand the reassurance. Kate closed her eyes and breathed out in a rush.

In a loud, tremoring voice she said, "Molly, bring Isabel to my parlour. I have seen little of her and I will spend time with her now." She swept off her cloak and handed it to me, then turned to the reverend. "I am sure you will excuse me, sir," she said. "I thank you for your service."

Smyth bowed.

Edward's smile was sardonic, though he coloured a little when Kate made him a formal curtsey without actually looking at him. Then she turned on her heel into the passageway, her silk skirts rustling wildly.

Every minute Smyth stayed felt like an hour. Kate and I sang songs and played finger games with Isabel, although our voices were too loud and our smiles too deliberate. Our eyes were constantly drawn to the place where the door was concealed.

I could not remove the picture from my mind of Makepeace sitting in the darkness behind the panelling only a few yards away. It was bizarre. It did not seem possible that he was there and Edward was casually showing a Lutheran over the house, a man who would surely alert his bishop if he suspected a priest was being housed here. Even the smell of incense in the chapel could draw suspicion. I had heard of families held for days while their home was ransacked, turned upside down in the search for hiding places. Bad enough if the holes were empty. I tried not to think of what happened when they found somebody. I did not think much of Makepeace as a man, that much is true, but he was still a priest – at least, I thought so at that time.

When Isabel grew bored of songs, she sat on the floor and chattered to her doll, rocking it like a baby and teaching it to dance. Her nonsense was precious in a way it never had been before. Kate smiled down at her through a slippery mouth. It made me tear up and my chin tremble all over again.

I wanted so much to speak to Kate about Harry. Perhaps she wanted to speak about him too. I do not think Makepeace could have heard us, not if we were careful, but the words would not come for either of us and so we sat in silence, watching and listening to Isabel, but also watching and listening for any noise behind the wainscot.

After what seemed like hours, I heard distant voices in the hall. One was Edward's, but louder than usual. The other was Smyth's, using the low tone of one showing compassion to the bereaved. The voices came closer. My heart thudded louder, so loud I was sure it would give me away. Kate seized my hand and squeezed it in a kind of spasm. Her face was taut.

The door opened. Kate snatched back her hand. Edward came into the room, followed by the parson, who sidled uncomfortably into the room. I rose from my stool and bobbed a wobbly curtsey, all the while seething on the inside. Kate was trembling all over.

"My dear," said Edward, making an extravagant bow. "Reverend Smyth is leaving, but he wishes to pay his respects first." Kate stared at Edward. So did I. He was ruddy in the face and had the motions of someone attempting to stand straight and keep their face under control without managing it. His breath was heavy with wine.

Kate blushed deeply and I felt embarrassed for her. Smyth looked sideways. She mumbled a few words at him. He bowed, said some words of condolence, and backed out of the room as fast as he could.

Through his drunken fog Edward saw Kate's tortured expression. He frowned momentarily, then squared his jaw and swaggered after Smyth.

The door was no sooner closed than Kate put her head in her hands and began to sob. I tried to take her hand but she waved me away. In broken words she told me to follow and make sure that Smyth was gone.

Before I had time to move, more footsteps approached the room. Lord Sherbourne entered first, looking grim. Then Kate's mother, her mouth a thin line. She cast severe eyes on Kate, who sucked in deep breaths and held them to stop her sobs. I stood up and backed away to the window. Last into the room was Ned.

"For God's sake, get him out of there!" Lady Sherbourne snapped at Ned. She grasped Isabel's hand firmly and ushered her out of the room.

Ned went straight to the wall next to the fireplace, counted along and then down the panels, and bent his knees to get purchase under the correct piece of moulding. There was a thud and Ned stepped away holding the section of panelling.

Kate's father stepped forward and turned the key in the little door. The door creaked open. Warm air billowed out, smelling of dust and neglect. There was no movement. Makepeace's arm hung loose in his lap. His body sagged against the wall. I caught Ned's eye, my eyes wide with horror. His were the same. What if we had killed him?

Edward sauntered into the parlour, swigging from a fresh bottle. He leaned against the wall and looked with amused interest at Makepeace's torso in the dark hole. The glares from Kate's parents did not seem to affect him. He did not look at Kate, whose gaze was fixed on the slumped body.

Ned moved first. He knelt by the door and peered in. Kate's father shook himself, then bent to look in as well.

"Father?" said Lord Sherbourne. "Father, can you hear me?"

Makepeace was entirely still. I think I may have held my breath. I began wondering how we would explain this. Questions would be asked.

A groan came from the priest hole. Makepeace's fingers moved. The room let out a collective sigh, except for Edward. He took a great glug of wine from his bottle, wiped his mouth with the back of his hand, then smirked and crossed his arms. Makepeace gradually eased himself onto his side and got himself onto his hands and knees, head out of the door.

It was indecent to see him reduced to crawling, yet I could not look away. He must have been wearing his vestments when Ned dragged him away from the chapel and was unable to untangle his legs properly, confused by the problem as a drunkard would be. He looked down his body and shuffled around. Nobody spoke. None of us moved to help him. It felt impossible to intrude.

Eventually, he got out of the hole, planted his hands on the floor and pushed himself upright just like Isabel did. Cobwebs clung to his hair and clothes. The shock of seeing this was replaced by an overwhelming urge to laugh. I couldn't laugh now. I mustn't. Thankfully for me, the colour of Makepeace's skin cut off this urge. It was as pale as Harry's had been when he was laid in his coffin. In places he was blue. He looked risen from the dead.

Makepeace staggered. Ned caught him and held him up. I dragged a chair behind him and he collapsed unceremoniously onto it, where he swayed and slurred. His gaze was unfocused like that of a man who had been in his cups all day.

Edward snorted. Then he chuckled. Then his shoulders began to shake and he laughed aloud, pointing at Makepeace and clutching his belly. The whole room turned to look at him, aghast. Even Makepeace swivelled his head in his direction.

"Edward!" said Kate. She had begun to cry again. "Edward, stop."

Edward laughed harder.

Then Makepeace stood up. His face was ugly, pale and twisted.

"You!" he shouted. "Whoreson!" He lurched towards Edward, fists ready to swing. Kate screamed.

Edward had more of his senses about him than Makepeace. He easily saw the fist coming. It was slow and off-target and Edward side-stepped. His bottle fell to the floor where it smashed and turned into a spreading puddle of glass shards.

Makepeace came for Edward again, his eyes like those of a maddened bull. Rather than dodging again, Edward squared himself and caught the other man with his fist as he came forward, plum across the bridge of Makepeace's nose.

There was a sickening squelch of gristle and blood. Makepeace staggered, hands clutching his nose. He moaned incoherently, backed up against the wall and slid down it. Blood seeped between his fingers, dark and thick.

Makepeace did not attend supper. I took food to his room, where he was staunching his broken nose. He did not speak to me and I had nothing to say. I took away the pile of rags he had stained red, dumped them in the scullery, and got back to the dining room.

The mood amongst the family was no better. Everyone was quiet and surly looks were thrown around the table. Edward had sobered up. Kate hardly ate and spent the time turning her wedding ring.

The meal was almost over when Edward broke the silence.

"I shall go to London, Kate," he said. "I would like you to come with me, but I shall not insist."

Kate seemed to struggle with what she wanted to say. Eventually, she said, "When?"

"Tomorrow. Or the day after, perhaps."

"So soon?" she said. "But Jane will not be out of bed for a while."

"I am not asking you to bring Jane. She will be looked after very well here. She is going to live – you heard Doctor Phillips."

Kate turned to her father. Her eyes pleaded for his help.

Lord Sherbourne tried. "But your London house is all shut up. You won't find servants to open it at this short notice. Especially not now. Everyone is celebrating."

"Then I shall find lodgings. *The Swan* is a good house. And I shall only need Ned with me. And you –" he said, nodding at Kate "– you can manage with Molly, can't you?"

My stomach did a flip. Go to London... *now?* Jane needed me. And she needed Kate too. And Kate needed to be home with her girls. I waited on pins for Kate's answer.

"I think... I feel that I ought to remain home. I do not feel able to go to London," she said.

She held Edward's gaze bravely. Her chin wobbled only slightly. He observed her silently and his mouth grew pinched.

He drew back his chair suddenly and Kate jumped. "Very well, madam," he said, throwing his napkin on the table. "I shall go alone." He strode out of the room, calling for Ned.

My belly flips became a heavy stone in my gut. Ned and I were due to be married. The banns had been read. I bit my lip. It could wait, I supposed. What difference could a few extra weeks make?

CHAPTER NINE

They left for London early the next morning. Ned had the horses ready by daybreak, loaded with the very few things that men seem to need. I said goodbye outside, wrapped tightly in my shawl. Nobody else had come.

"Do you know when you'll be home?" I asked.

Ned shook his head. I looked at the ground and kicked at the gravel. He chuckled weakly. "Don't pull that face. If the wind changes you'll stay like it."

I didn't feel like laughing.

Edward strode out of the dark house, pulling on his gloves. He tutted at the two of us. "Say your farewells quickly. I want to be off."

Ned pulled me against his chest and I put my arms around his waist. "As soon as I'm home we'll be down that church, Moll," he said. "And I'll write if I'm able."

I nodded against his cloak, not trusting myself to speak. I'd either have cried or shouted at him. It wasn't his fault, I knew that, but I could hardly complain to Edward.

Ned kissed my forehead and I tipped my head up to be kissed again. He touched my lips lightly with his and smiled a wonky smile. Then he let me go.

Edward was already seated. His horse pawed the ground, just as impatient. Ned mounted quickly, nodded at me, and they were off. I watched until they were out of view, picked up my basket and stomped off to collect the eggs.

Time without Ned crawled by. I hoped that the visitors would leave after Twelfth Night, as their original plan had been. Kate would have done better to grieve without them, but Epiphany came and went and no travel arrangements were announced.

Jane left her bed ten days after her danger period was over. She convalesced in the chair in her room for several days. Then Kate and I took turns to persuade her to come downstairs. She claimed to be weaker than she really was, but it was impossible to be angry with her. She had lost a dear brother and the scars she had escaped with were numerous and fresh. She often ran her fingers over them anxiously. I wonder sometimes whether we would have won her over eventually had not Lady Sherbourne taken matters into her own hands. I also wonder whether things would have turned out as they did.

I was bringing Jane some food when Lady Sherbourne stopped me in the kitchen doorway.

"Put that down, Molly," she said. "Miss Jane will eat downstairs or she will not eat at all. Now come and help her dress fit to be seen."

Protest was impossible. The old lady marched up the stairs to Jane's room and I followed meekly.

She entered the room briskly. "This is enough moping

around, child. Molly will help you into your gown and you will eat with the family."

Jane's eyes widened. I longed to reach out to her but did not dare. She tried to speak and was cut off before a word could pass her lips.

"I mean it, Jane. You have to face the world sometime and it might as well be now," Lady Sherbourne said.

Tears sprang to Jane's eyes and she looked to me for reprieve. I bit my lip and stayed silent and still.

"For Heaven's sake, girl, don't look to Molly for help! You're strong enough to eat at the table and that's the end of the matter."

"But Grandmother, please," said Jane between sobs, touching her newly scarred face.

Lady Sherbourne seized Jane's shoulders and shook her. I stretched out an arm but my feet were rooted to the floor. Jane was shocked into silence, staring up at her grandmother.

Once she had her full attention, Lady Sherbourne let the girl go. There was no chair but the one Jane occupied. Lady Sherbourne glanced at the stool in the corner then pointedly at me. I hurried to fetch and place it near Jane.

Grandly as a queen upon a throne, she positioned herself on the stool and turned her head to Jane. "Do not ever behave in this way again. What has happened is truly terrible. I do not pretend to understand the will of God, but we must accept it. We must all accept the loss of Harry. You must accept the loss of your face.

"But you must also see that you have been spared your life and be grateful for it. You have strength, too, more than you know. You must live your life well, for all our sakes. Our menfolk are already convinced we are feeble-minded – there is no need to prove them right."

Jane watched her grandmother's face throughout. Her tears ceased and she sat up straight. At a gesture from Lady Sherbourne, I fetched Jane's gown from the closet and helped her into it. She held still for me to fasten the bodice and attach the sleeves. Lady Sherbourne applied some of her own white makeup to Jane's face.

"There," she said, showing Jane her handiwork in the looking glass. "You look like a proper young lady. No more hiding. Come downstairs."

Jane did indeed look quite different from the Jane of a few weeks ago, and not only because of the face paint. She held herself differently. Stiller, somehow. I offered her my arm to lean on. She went to take it but a look from her grandmother made her change her mind.

"No, Molly. I can manage," she said. Jane glanced back at Lady Sherbourne, who nodded brief approval.

I stood back and bobbed a curtsey, the first I had ever made to Jane. Lady Sherbourne turned to lead the way from the room, followed closely by her namesake. They both paused to draw themselves erect. The women of this family looked the world in the face.

Weeks and weeks passed and yet we heard nothing from London, until I had given up hope. Kate's parents and Makepeace hung on at Spicer Hall, always putting off their departure by another week. They meant well. At least, Lord and Lady Sherbourne meant well. Makepeace enjoyed exhorting Kate to leave off her grief, which he called excessive. But nobody could have expected the events that unfolded because they remained.

The weather began to thaw and the nights grew shorter. Lent began. It became clear that our visitors intended to stay until after Easter. Finally, a messenger arrived in the middle of the day with a letter for Kate. I opened the door to receive it, paid him and sent him around to Cook for some food.

The letter felt thick. I hoped there would be a few lines in there for me. Ned could pen his own words. I was proud to be promised to a man who could read *and* write. His writing wasn't elegant like Edward's, of course, but he got by. Perhaps he was coming home soon.

I gave the letter to Kate with a smile, sure it would cheer her up. She had barely left the house despite invitations from various acquaintances.

"At last," she said, and broke the seal. Sure enough, tucked inside her letter was a thinner one for me bearing Ned's spiky penmanship. I took it eagerly and trotted away to find a quiet corner.

My dearest Molly, it said. I was grinning already.

We are safe in London and are lodged at The Swan. I wish I had not had to leave you, but I hope you are well and that my father and all the family are well too. I do not know how long we will stay here. Sir Edward is in no hurry to leave.
I worry for him, Moll. Say nothing of this to anyone. He drinks too much and I fear he will do himself a mischief – in more ways than one. Some of the company he keeps alarms me. I do not mean women. His companions are

men with strange ideas. I will say no more, but I charge you
to keep our mistress close as I try to keep the master close.
As I have said, I do not know when we come home. I hope
it will not be long. Then we will marry.

Your own,
Ned

I read the letter twice and was as puzzled the second time as the first. What strange ideas? I folded it and, because I was alone, I kissed it, and I put it deep in my pocket. Then I took it out again. *Men with strange ideas. Not women.*

It couldn't be that. We would know already. Edward had only ever been interested in women. He loved Kate. And there was that silly girl for a while, Ellen. But then, Edward was not himself. Going off to London at a time like this. And that madness before it, having Smyth at the house.

I checked the letter once more. *He drinks too much.* Edward had been drinking when he broke Makepeace's nose. Did drink make men turn to other men sometimes? That didn't seem likely, but I didn't know for sure. I was missing something. What was Ned not saying?

My mind was a blank. I stared at the letter, searching for a clue. In the end, I tutted, folded it, and thrust it back in my pocket. Drat Ned and his short letters.

What sort of letter had Kate received, I wondered. On the pretext of checking the fire, I returned to the parlour. She had had her writing desk brought in and she hardly looked up from it. Her hand flew across the paper.

I lingered, poking at the edges of the fire.

"There is nothing wrong with the fire, Molly," she said. "You can leave now."

Kate would normally have asked if I had any message to pass on to Ned. She was kind like that. But this was not one of those types of letters, clearly. With no choice in the matter, I went away.

A short while later, Kate called for me again. Her letter was carefully folded and sealed so that nobody could peek at a word of it. I held my hand out for it and was surprised when she kept it close to her.

"Is the man in the kitchen?" she asked.

I said that he was.

"Tell him he must be back on his horse in five minutes. I will give him this when he is mounted," she said.

"Tonight, madam?" I said, glancing out of the window.

"There are several hours of riding time left. I want this letter to reach London as soon as possible."

This was not Kate's normal hospitality. I paused too long for her patience.

"Do I have to repeat myself, Molly?" she snapped.

"No, madam," I said, and went to the kitchen to chivvy the messenger.

After supper, in the parlour, Lord Sherbourne played Makepeace at chess, while the ladies worked with their embroidery and I darned some stockings. Jane's pink little tongue stuck out with the concentration of making the stitches well. Lady Sherbourne examined her work occasionally and so far had had no cause to scold her. It made me smile to see Jane recovering so well. It was still strange, though, for her to be made up in white paint. A proper little lady.

I also smiled to myself at the new shape of Makepeace's nose, sneaking a look at it now and again. I wondered if it still hurt. The swelling had subsided, but his nose would be ugly for the rest of his life. He caught me looking once or twice. I decided I didn't care much.

Makepeace had recovered his composure now Edward had left. He frequently disapproved of the ungodliness he saw around him just as he had for twenty years or more, and gave everyone plenty of advice. Lady Sherbourne listened and nodded to his words. Lord Sherbourne, though, had begun to crease his brow when Makepeace offered criticism. Once he asked if Makepeace's view was indeed the view of the Church or his personal opinion. Since then, the priest addressed Kate's mother rather than her father.

This particular evening, however, he was quiet, concentrating on the chess.

Kate was distracted, often staring off into the fire, holding her needle in mid-stitch. I wondered if she was thinking of Harry or of her letter from Edward. I knew something was preying on her mind.

The men finished their game. Makepeace bowed humbly to his opponent yet his smirk betrayed his delight at his victory. He tried to cover it by taking a drink.

Lord Sherbourne pushed back his chair and stretched out his shoulders. I watched him surreptitiously over my darning. He saw Kate frozen, her needle poised to make a stitch. He rubbed his beard and gazed at her, then seemed to arrive at a decision.

"Kate," he said. His voice was cheerful and he had dressed

his face in a smile. Kate started. "Did I hear right? You received a letter today?"

Kate's hand moved automatically to her pocket. Then she snatched it away again.

"How is Edward?" her father continued.

"He is well," Kate said. She looked from her father to her mother, who had also lifted her head from her work. Kate's blush spread across her cheeks.

I paid close attention while trying to appear engaged. Everyone else looked at her expectantly. Even Makepeace looked at Kate with keen interest. He normally paid her little attention. I felt a prickling of my skin, like a warning.

Kate reluctantly added, "He does not know when he will return. Not yet. He has some... matters... to attend to. People to talk to about... things."

"Things?" Lady Sherbourne said.

"Yes," Kate said. "Some acquaintances who live in London." Her blush filled her entire face.

She had never been any use at telling lies. Too honest for her own good. I wondered if she was worried about the same thing as I was. I wondered if Edward had been more explicit than Ned.

But I had got something wrong. I was missing something. A married man would hardly write and tell his wife that he preferred the company of other men.

Kate briefly touched her pocket again. She smiled at her mother, father and Jane in turn, then made a great display of being industrious with her embroidery. Her parents glanced at each other, Lord Sherbourne shrugged, and Jane looked around at everyone in an effort to understand what was happening. Then everyone got back to their activities.

I frowned at my darning, then put it down, wondering what

Edward had written about. I was not the only one whose mind was no longer on what was in my hands. Makepeace rolled the black queen between his thumb and forefinger, watching Kate while she sewed vigorously, his head tipped over like a curious raven.

CHAPTER TEN

Later that evening I helped Kate into her night shift and began putting away her day clothes.

"Wait, Molly," she said, reaching into the pocket of her gown. She withdrew the letter from Edward. It was flatter than when it was delivered, settled into its folds. She had opened it many times.

Kate climbed into bed while I continued to tidy. She sat up and angled the letter to catch the light from her candle. I turned slyly so I could watch her. While she read, she nibbled at her fingernails. She hadn't done that in years.

I spoke cautiously. "I hope your husband is well, madam."

Kate looked up from her letter and seemed surprised to see me there. "Oh. Yes. He is well, I think."

I turned back to my folding, and then she said, in a forced, bright tone, "And Ned, too? What was in his letter to you?"

I felt the tables turned against me and I reddened a little. "Not much, madam. Just to say he misses me."

"Nothing else?"

Drat. It was my own fault for bringing it up. And now I had paused too long and she knew Ned had said something else.

"Of course, if it is a personal matter, I will not pry, Molly. You will soon be married, after all."

"I hope so. I hope he can come home soon... I mean..." My words began to trip over each other. "I only mean, we have waited so long already... I'm sorry, I didn't mean to say that..."

Kate held up a hand and gave a little smile. A real one, not the fixed one of earlier when she was avoiding telling her parents about her letter.

"I only mean to ask, did Ned mention my husband in his letter?"

Her eyes seemed to see right into me and know every thought. I stopped myself blurting out everything I had been fearing and wondering, but I had to think of something to say.

"Yes, Ned did mention him briefly, madam. Just once. Just to tell me that... he is worried for Sir Edward."

"Worried for him?" Kate's face clouded. "Worried in what way?"

I chose my words carefully. "That he might be mixing with the wrong crowd."

Kate's expression sharpened. "What crowd? What people?"

"Men who drink," I said.

I braced myself for further questioning but Kate visibly relaxed. Ned commenting on Edward's drinking was nothing compared to – well, compared to whatever she was worrying about.

"He has taken the loss of Harry very hard," Kate said.

I nodded. I knew if I spoke I would say the wrong thing.

"I want to help him, Molly, but I don't know how."

Kate seemed so young suddenly. I wished I could reach out

and hug her tightly, tell her everything would come out well. I wished I knew that it would. She reached out for my hand. I gave it to her and stroked her fingers with my thumb.

"Losing Harry is hard on you too," I ventured. I couldn't say that Edward was selfish, running off to London because Harry had died. I couldn't say that he ought to be here. I couldn't even say I was angry that Edward was keeping Ned in town so he could get drunk, instead of letting us get married. I had to swallow all that down, no matter how it burned.

"Sometimes I forget, just for a moment. When I remember, it hurts all over again." Kate motioned for me to pass her a handkerchief. I took my own from my pocket as well and dabbed at my eyes. "But Harry is safe now. He is with God. I must believe that," she said.

"Of course. He could not be anywhere else. Such a sweet child. Purgatory is not for him."

A strange look passed across Kate's face, and she opened her mouth to say more, then closed it. Her eyes slid sideways. "Yes, that's it." She folded the letter, tucked in all the edges, and handed it to me. "Molly, put this away for me," she said.

Kate's writing desk had been returned to its usual spot in the bedroom. It was a beautiful object, silky smooth to touch, with a sloping top, several drawers, and special compartments for quills and ink. It was a gift from Edward early in their marriage. Kate had been so excited the day he presented it to her.

I opened the drawer where she kept the letters she had received and slid it onto the top of the little pile. Then I bid her goodnight and took my candle through the connecting door to my own little room.

I especially remembered Kate in my prayers that night. I also prayed that He would see both her man and mine home soon.

The next day was a washing day. There were beds to strip and remake, and even with extra help from the village – the girls had come back now the sickness had left – it took every female pair of hands to get it done.

I came out of Makepeace's room with a bundle of linen in my arms and jumped when he appeared in front of me. He looked at me without blinking as he always did. I forced myself to meet his gaze. It made the hairs on the nape of my neck prickle.

"Ah, Molly. I hoped I would see you."

Me? He had never hoped to see me before, I was certain of *that*. I was below his notice unless it was at confession, and then I was a chore, just as I viewed these stinking sheets.

I must have been staring because he smiled. At least, the corners of his mouth lifted. I managed to speak eventually. "What can I do for you, Mister Farendon?"

"I have taken the liberty of looking for some writing paper in Sir Edward's study but I cannot find any. Perhaps it is locked up. Could you help me, Molly?" he said.

I think this was the longest non-religious speech Makepeace had ever addressed to me. It was certainly the politest.

Flustered, I looked around for somewhere to dump his dirty linen.

"I see you are busy," he said. "Perhaps you know where there is some paper kept closer than the study. Does Lady Spicer keep her own store?"

I was puzzled by his considerateness but too busy to stop and think what it might mean. Later, I would wish with all my heart that I had.

"I believe she keeps a small supply in her writing desk, sir. I shall ask her."

And like a fool I foisted the linen bundle on a passing girl and trotted down the passageway to the nursery.

Kate was holding Isabel on her knee and talking to Margaret about new shoes for the child. She must have grown again. I explained my errand. Kate was reluctant to leave and told me where in her desk I could find the paper. And so I went next to Kate's room, opened the little desk and found a sheet of paper. As a second thought, I also found a small bottle of ink and a couple of pens.

Makepeace was close by again when I came out, but this time I was half expecting him and did not jump.

"I thought you might also be without these, sir?" I said, showing him the ink and pens.

He paused for a hair's breadth of a moment. Then he said smoothly, "Yes, I am indeed. Thank you, Molly."

I handed the materials over, bobbed at him and tried to get back to supervising the girls' bed-stripping. He seemed determined to keep me in conversation, though. I began to feel less puzzled and more irritated.

"Lady Spicer spends much of her time indoors, does she not?" he said.

"Of late, yes. My lady does not generally take the air in the rain." I tried to keep my tone bland. I know I didn't manage it. My face was probably scathing in any case. Ned always said I couldn't hide my thoughts.

Makepeace chose to ignore my rudeness. Another warning sign, but I did not see the danger coming. Perhaps I willingly fooled myself that he had not noticed.

"It would do her some good to take a walk today. The weather looks promising. Will you suggest it to her?"

I glanced out of the window. It was not actually raining, if that was what he meant. And this concern for Kate's welfare was a new and baffling phenomenon. It was odd to hear him express concern for *anyone's* welfare. Perhaps he was beginning to think about how people saw him and had resolved to try harder.

"Yes, I will," I said.

The corners of his lips turned upwards again and he headed for the stairs. I frowned, then shuddered. I decided I preferred Makepeace when he was exhorting me to confess my sins. A moment later, though, I set my mind back on the care of the linen. These village girls had to be watched carefully.

As it turned out, Kate decided to go outside without me suggesting it. The sun was as high in the sky as it was going to get and it wasn't very damp so she, Jane and Margaret took Isabel outside in the grounds.

Isabel squealed to be outside. I watched her from the bushes where I was checking how the linen was drying. She resisted every attempt to make her walk decently and flung herself around the grassy walkway. Kate ceased trying to keep Isabel by her side and instead watched her indulgently as she tumbled around like a performer. Jane giggled at the show. Even Kate laughed once. It was music to my ears.

I collected the laundry that was ready for airing by the fire. Inside, I stripped the drying racks of the warm sheets, put the cold ones on them, and summoned a girl to help me put the best sheets back on Lady Sherbourne's bed.

We were on the half landing at the turn in the stairs when a door upstairs clicked shut. I looked up as Makepeace passed the head of the stairs. They were all family rooms down that passageway. His was the other way.

The girl and I went into Lady Sherbourne's room and made it up between us. When we were done, I sent her back to the kitchens while I stayed to remove a few new spiderwebs. Then I decided I might as well dust the rest of the rooms too, since I had to wait for more sheets to be safe to put on the beds.

Kate's room was soon cleaned and tidied. Just the bed to make up. I cast my eyes around to check I hadn't missed anything and they fell on the writing desk. I dismissed an awful thought from my head, but it came back stronger. I was ashamed of the urge, yet my curiosity needled me to such a degree that I could not turn away.

My heart quivered. I opened the door a little and checked the passage was empty. I held my breath in order to hear even distant footsteps. There was only silence. I closed the door – the handle squeaked – and turned the lock as quietly as I could. Then I tiptoed – I don't know why I tiptoed, but I did – to the writing desk.

My fingers trembled. I pulled out the little drawer and took the letter from the top of the pile. The need to check over my shoulder seized me. Idiot.

I knew I ought to have put it back and left the room, but I unfolded the paper and read. It began,

My Dear Daughter,
Thank you for your invitation to spend the coming
Season with you and your Husband. Your Father and I
will be delighted...

I frowned, put this letter to one side and looked again at the small pile of letters in the drawer. They were all too small. It was none of them. I checked the other little compartments of the desk. If I hadn't done this, there might still have been time to prevent what happened.

I was examining the drawer of letters again to see if the one I wanted could have slipped behind somehow, when I heard a yell of *Mamma!* from the passageway. My blood began pounding in my ears. Little footsteps pattered. Kate's voice followed after, calling *Yes* to Isabel. I folded the letter from Kate's mother, my fingers suddenly slow and clumsy, popped it back on the top of the pile, and closed the drawer and the top of the desk.

The door handle squeaked and I spun around to face it. I saw it sit upright again and there was silence. Then Kate's voice came. "Hallo?"

I fairly ran to unlock the door. Kate stared at me. I must have looked a sight – bright red, I suspect. "Madam..." I said. "I was... I'm sorry, I was..."

"Why lock the door, Molly?" Kate said, coming into her room. There was no other question, really.

"I... forgot I had." *Pathetic.*

"But why lock it at all?"

"I... needed to use the chamber pot."

Kate's brow creased.

"While I was cleaning I had to... go." I waved in the general direction of my adjoining room. Well. The Queen's Spymaster would not ever want to recruit *me*, would he? But I was committed to it now so it would have to do. "And I forgot to unlock it again afterwards." My words tailed off at the end and I bit my lip. I felt, and probably looked, ridiculous.

Isabel bounced into the room and right up to me, tugging on my skirt. I was never more glad to see her.

"Moll!" she said. "We saw a skirrel! It had hairy ears and it ran and ran right up a tree!"

"Did you?" I said. I crouched to be the same height as her. "How lovely. It must be out looking for its treasure."

Isabel gasped. "Like rubies and emrulds?" She turned to Kate. "Mamma, let's go find the treasure!"

Kate laughed. "Maybe we'll look tomorrow, if it's fine. Go with Margaret now. It's time to wash your hands before dinner."

"Dinner!" Isabel shouted and ran into Margaret's skirts in the doorway. Margaret bent down, whispered to Isabel, and turned her around so she could perform her funny curtsey to her mother.

The two of them went hand in hand along to the nursery. Kate went to her own washstand. I spied my chance to leave and took it.

CHAPTER ELEVEN

I guessed that Kate had moved the letter somewhere less obvious than her writing desk. She was right to, as it had turned out. A deep shame filled me the rest of the day. If Kate couldn't trust me to respect her privacy, what good was I to her?

Makepeace was nowhere to be seen at dinner. According to Old Ned, he had taken a horse from the stables.

"Risky," Lord Sherbourne commented, tearing his bread.

"Well, yes," Kate's mother said. "What is he thinking of?"

Her husband shrugged into his plate by way of an answer. There was meat at the table and no Makepeace to look on disapprovingly if he ate his fill. Lady Sherbourne tutted and turned to Kate to seek an answer. Kate shook her head apologetically. Jane kept her eyes lowered modestly.

Makepeace wasn't much for exercise. A stroll in the grounds was usually enough. Plus, the weather had taken a turn for the worse. Chancing being seen and recognised by Reverend Smyth for the sake of a ride in the drizzle was downright odd. I had felt queasy ever since I'd escaped from Kate's room. My mother always said a guilty conscience was its own punishment. But now my gut tightened. I remembered Makepeace passing the head of the stairs earlier. From the family rooms.

I became aware of silence in the dining room. Lady Sherbourne was staring at me. Kate looked at me strangely.

"What is the matter with the girl?" Kate's mother asked the room. She tapped her cup with a finger.

I blushed, probably crimson, and hurried to fill it.

Makepeace didn't return until around three in the afternoon. I lingered in the upstairs rooms at the front of the house, waiting to see him reappear. I don't know what I expected to learn from watching the man dismount a horse, but I had to see him get home. Inventing jobs to do in those rooms also meant I could put off facing Kate. I knew it was cowardly while I did it, and it made me bad-tempered. The village girls were still doing chores in the house. One or other of them would bother me with some trivial problem, until I snapped and scolded the unlucky one who asked me one question too many. She went away with tears in her eyes. I was immediately sorry for it but was glad none of them approached me again.

Every time I heard the crunch of hooves on gravel – or imagined I did – I slipped to the window and peeked around the edge of the curtain. By the time Makepeace trotted his horse through the grounds I was a bag of shredded nerves. Perhaps my fears made me perceive it this way, but the way he threw the reins to the boy and walked into the house was different. By habit he was a creeper and a slinker. Now he swaggered.

The queasy misgivings in my belly congealed into certainty. He had the letter. I knew he did. But what had it told him? More

importantly, what could he do with the knowledge? What had he already done? Had I been braver or cleverer, I would have gone to Kate and told her everything – Ned's concern about Edward's friends with strange ideas, my trespassing on her privacy, the missing letter, and who I suspected had taken it. If I was right and Makepeace had already taken action, then our fates were already sealed, but by going to Kate I might have saved myself a greater humiliation than a private confession.

That evening Makepeace was in good spirits, at least compared with his usual humour. Kate didn't say a word to me at supper-time. I might as well have been a stick of furniture. She must have gone looking for her letter and found it gone. I could not stop fidgeting, which seemed to amuse Makepeace further, especially when Lady Sherbourne scolded me.

"For Heaven's sake, Molly, stand still!" she said. "Kate, don't you have anyone more capable to serve us? She's spilt more food on the cloth than she has put in the bowls."

Kate looked at me finally. "Molly, go down to the kitchen. We will shift for ourselves. Come back later and clean up." Then she looked back at her meal. Kate's mother gave her a surprised but impressed smile.

I was stunned, although I had no right to be. Kate ignored my curtsey. On my way out of the dining room, Makepeace's lips turned upwards. His eyes slid towards me for a fraction of a second. I just made it into the passageway before my eyes blurred.

It was my own fault. I had been with Kate so long I had become used to sharing her worries and joys, big or small. I had forgotten I was a servant. I could not pinpoint when it had begun but it had crept up on me and taken me over. I had thought I was so clever and wise but I was just as foolish as I had been at thirteen.

I did not go to the kitchen. It would be full of servants. The other servants, I meant. I didn't want Ned to get out of me what was wrong. Instead, I slipped into the yard through the scullery and took some shaking breaths, forcing myself to make each breath deeper than the last. The night was damp and misty, and utterly silent. The chickens had long since been shut up in their house. I closed my eyes and let the fine rain wet my face, taking the time to think.

My heart gradually slowed and I stopped trembling. I came to a decision. I would do what I ought to have done straight away. The first opportunity I had alone with Kate, I would tell her exactly what I had done, make my apology, and warn her that her letter – and whatever it contained, for it was none of my business – might be in the hands of someone who wished her husband ill.

I knew my best chance would come at the end of the day when I helped Kate undress. On my way to her room, I ran over the words I wanted to say and how I would say them. Kate had never been unkind. She would listen. I took a deep breath and knocked on the door. Kate's muffled voice said, "Come in."

My hope died when I saw Kate was not alone. Lady Sherbourne sat in Kate's chair, her fingers curled around the carved ends of the armrests. It was like being on trial for my life before a queen, and I began trembling again. I clasped my hands behind my back to try to still them. My eyes jerked from her stony face to Kate's and back. I opened my mouth, although it wasn't to say the words I had practised. I don't know what I was trying to say.

"Don't speak, Molly," Lady Sherbourne said, raising a single finger. I closed my mouth. She continued, "The only reason you are still in this house is that my daughter is mistress here rather than I."

Her nostrils flared and her mouth pinched. She was getting into her stride. I had witnessed Lady Sherbourne's dismissal of servants. It was always brief and brutal. She began to say more but true to her word about Kate being in charge, she stopped herself. She turned briefly to Kate, acknowledging with a tilt of her head Kate's prerogative to pass sentence.

My chin began wobbling and I clenched my jaw hard. I resigned myself to being turned out of doors that night. My mind whirled with thoughts about whose mercy I might throw myself on. Whose roof might I sleep under? From there my thoughts leapt to where I could go to begin again. My aunt wouldn't take me, that was for sure. Not with my mother employed by Lord Sherbourne. Then a worse thought occurred. What about Ned? Would he still want to marry me? Would he leave with me or keep his life here?

In the time it took for me to turn to Kate and drop my gaze from her face, all my hopes of becoming a happy bride crumbled into dust. I waited for the blow to fall.

"I am going to ask you a question," Kate said. I nodded miserably. "Did you take my letter from my husband from my writing desk?" Her voice was hurt.

I made myself look into her eyes. A very quiet, "No," came out. Even that stuck in my throat. I was in great danger of not being able to say any more. If that happened I was doomed.

Lady Sherbourne made a noise of disgust and disbelief. Kate looked at me and her eyes pleaded. Anger did not come easily to her. I wished at that moment that it did. I wished she would shout at me, slap me even, if only she would not look so... disappointed.

Panic took hold of me and sobs rose from my chest. I began to blurt out everything. Ned's letter. My worries. The laundry. Me giving away to Makepeace the whereabouts of the writing desk when I gave him writing materials. My curiosity. The missing letter.

I doubt it made sense. I know it did not come in any kind of order. Indeed, Lady Sherbourne's expression showed no patience. Kate seemed to try to understand me, bless her, and even placed a hand on her mother's shoulder to ask her to let me finish while she picked out the intelligible scraps from my words.

"So," I managed to say between gulps of air, "I haven't... got it. I swear... I haven't seen it. I did... try... to find it, yes... but it was... gone."

"You see how this looks bad, Molly?" Kate said. "You were very strange earlier... with the door locked. If you have my letter, I just need to have it back. It is important that nobody else sees it."

I was aware Kate was trying her best for me. Most mistresses would have had me thrown out by now rather than seek to understand. I owed her total honesty, for that alone, so I took a few deep breaths and made a massive effort to speak calmly.

"That was when I tried to find it. I am sorry. I shouldn't have. But I swear I am telling the truth. It wasn't there," I said.

Kate held my gaze. She was normally an open book. I was used to reading every emotion that passed across her face, but I could not tell what she was thinking at that moment. She had closed off her mind to me.

Lady Sherbourne broke the silence with a loud tut. "Enough of this nonsense," she said, slapping the arm of the chair.

"Katherine... you were determined to deal with this. You said yourself it had to be Molly. You heard what Father Makepeace said, too. He saw her putting a letter into her pocket!"

It was a few moments before I understood. At first, my muddled mind played tricks on me and I thought he had seen me reading my own note from Ned and reported it in error as Kate's stolen one. But he had not made a mistake. He knew exactly where Kate's letter was because he had taken it. And he had made sure that I was in line for the blame. I felt my anger against him rise, but then it turned inwards against me. Lady Sherbourne would always take Makepeace's word, but it was my own fault that Kate believed him too. I was so ashamed.

Kate's mother stood up and began to pace. Her voice rose. "You see? No good comes from educating a servant. If Molly could not read, she would not be interested in matters beyond her own business."

I did not feel angry. She was right. I would have done better to remain ignorant. I had been so proud of knowing my letters but it had only brought trouble. I hung my head in silence.

Kate did not speak for some time. Her mother's skirts rustled as she moved about and she harrumphed and muttered under her breath, but Kate remained still. I felt her eyes on me.

After an eternity she said, "Molly." I looked up. Her eyes were softened but still wary. "I am going to search your room. If I do not find my letter, I will believe you."

A wave of gratitude swept over me. Before I could feel much relief, though, Lady Sherbourne interjected again. "She will have burned it by now."

"I do not see why she would do that, Mother. I do not see why Molly would take it away at all, if it comes to that. Why would she not read it and put it back? I would not suspect a thing," said Kate.

My mouth fell open. This was the first time I had heard Kate contradict her mother's opinion outright. I risked a tiny sideways glance at Lady Sherbourne. She was torn between frustration and the logic of Kate's words.

Kate still faced her mother. I held my silence, waiting for my fate.

When Lady Sherbourne spoke at last, I thought I detected grudging respect – not for me but for Kate. "Very well. Let us search Molly's room. And this room too. If the letter is in either, she goes."

Kate was silent, thinking. She looked only at her mother. I was helpless. Very slowly, she nodded.

The search felt like it lasted hours. From where I was instructed to remain in Kate's room, I heard Kate and her mother lift my mattress between them. My gratitude to Kate shifted into further shame. Then a more terrible dread crept up on me. What if the letter was there in my room? My door had no lock. It would be so easy to put it under my sheets or inside my wooden box.

I imagined a shout of triumph from Lady Sherbourne. I pictured her returning through the adjoining door waving an incriminating document at me and shouting at me to collect my belongings because I was to leave this instant. I saw Kate's hurt, pale face as she followed in silent agreement.

My heart pounded. I clenched and unclenched my fingers. After an eternity they came back into Kate's chamber. Kate looked into drawers. Lady Sherbourne forgot about her aching bones and rummaged amongst Kate's gowns, whipped aside the

CHAPTER TWELVE

Two days went by. Makepeace looked only once in my direction. He appeared disappointed I was still in the house, but he shook this off and returned to ignoring me as much as ever. He even went about with a spring in his step. At supper he took wine instead of ale. He smiled into the distance rather than paying attention to conversations, and he seemed not to notice Lord Sherbourne's healthy appetite.

Kate also observed the change. She looked at him often and with more fear than ever. Once, he noticed her watching him. Instead of the solemn gaze with which he normally observed Kate, he arched his eyebrows and turned his mouth up into a cold smile. Kate did not raise the subject of the letter again with me – not then – and of course I could not mention it, but it hung unspoken in the air.

Night fell on the second day. Kate permitted me to bring my mending into the parlour and take up my usual spot so I could serve them and stoke the fire. I took this as a step toward forgiveness. Lady Sherbourne tutted and glared at me. I felt a fresh wave of embarrassment, but Kate pretended not to hear, and so I stayed.

We had not been seated long before a heavy knock came at the door. I jumped. Kate and Jane gasped. Lord Sherbourne exclaimed loudly. Only Makepeace did not appear disturbed. He looked up from the chess table like an expectant bird. His eyes gleamed and the corners of his mouth turned upwards. I did not mark how strange it was that the person with the most to fear would welcome a visit after dark.

Then everyone – or everyone except Makepeace – moved at once. Lady Sherbourne gestured for me to open up the priest hole. Lord Sherbourne stood ready to take the panelled section from me. Kate put herself in everybody's way and fidgeted, rubbing and twisting her wedding ring feverishly. She paled so greatly that I worried she was about to faint. Jane crept around the back of her chair, watching our activity with an open mouth. Only afterwards did it occur to me that nobody thought to take her out of the room. Three months ago she had been a child. Now she was grown.

The hiding place was clean. That was one of my earliest jobs after the business with Reverend Smyth paying a visit. I opened the little door and stood to one side. Makepeace stood calmly. It struck me finally that something was off. He approached the priest hole, not serenely, not showing courage in the face of danger, but arrogantly, as if courage was unnecessary. Yet Kate was a bundle of nerves and had been for some time.

Before Makepeace submitted to the indignity of squeezing himself into the dark space, he paused and met Kate's eyes. He looked down his nose at her, then nodded slowly, his head on one side like a bird and his lips turned upwards. She stared up at him dumbly. My thought that something was wrong became a heavy sickness in my gut.

Then the moment was over and he sat on the floor to manoeuvre himself backwards into the hole. Another knock sounded at the door, more urgent than before. A voice sounded outside. The words were muffled but the meaning was unmistakable. Someone demanded entry.

Several servants loitered at the edge of the hall closest to the kitchen. None of them had the authority to answer the door at night. Curious faces peeked out of the gloom, a few rushlights amongst them.

"If you are done with your chores, go to bed," I told them. My voice was loud, covering my jitters with a scolding. They shuffled away reluctantly, and the only light left was my single candle.

Again a fist pounded on the door. The words that followed were those we dreaded.

"Open in the name of the Queen!"

I crossed the hall on shaking legs. My candle quivered in my hand and the flame danced insanely. I shaded it with my hand. The knocking came again.

"Coming!" I called out. I didn't sound like me.

The key was on its hook. My fingers trembled and I held it tight. A soft leathery sound came from behind me. I gasped and looked over my shoulder, then sighed to see Lord Sherbourne buckling his sword belt around him. His wife gave him the light of her candle, her face grim.

I fumbled the key into the lock, breathing hard.

"Come on, come on!" said the gruff voice of a stranger on the other side.

I opened the door a little. The unmistakable sound of steel being unsheathed rang out, and the door was pushed from the outside.

The hall filled with men, perhaps half a dozen, dragging in mud and threat with them. Their leader looked me up and down and stepped close. I shrank from his breath, but another man stood behind me, holding a lantern over my shoulder, and I could not get away. My blood came loud in my ears.

"I must speak with Lady Spicer. Where is your mistress?" he said. A London man.

I could not find my voice. My eyes flicked from side to side. Wherever they landed they met with cold steel, either the sword of the man doing the talking or the knives and daggers of his men. The candle shook violently in my hand. He came closer still, leering down at me and breathing his foul breath over me until I was forced to turn my face away.

"Where is she?" My heart beat faster still. Bodies pressed closer around me.

"What do you want with my daughter?" came Lord Sherbourne's voice. The crowd of bodies around me shifted. The lantern next to my face lifted away and I found my breath again.

The leader of the men switched his focus to Lord Sherbourne. All but one of them followed, shadowing his movements. The one directly behind me stayed there and I edged away to get him where I could see him. He was a ratty little man, and none too clean. He noticed my distaste and grinned unpleasantly with dirty teeth.

"I said, what do you want with my daughter? She is not coming out here in the cold for the likes of you," said Lord Sherbourne. "And what the devil do you mean by barging in here?" He had drawn himself up to his full height, hand on his sword. He had never been a tall man but was broad. Even now, past sixty, he still had most of his strength.

The leader made to step towards him. Lord Sherbourne sharply drew his sword just an inch and the man reconsidered. Lady Sherbourne did not move from her husband's side.

"Who are you?" she said. "I wonder if you realise to whom you are speaking." I marvelled at her control and the way she managed to look down her nose at these rough men despite being a foot shorter than their leader.

"Oh, yes, milady," said the one in charge. He looked over his shoulder at his men and sniggered, who followed suit with humourless chuckles. Stupidly, I was most appalled that these men had not removed their hats.

"I suppose it don't matter if we see his wife or not," the man continued, jerking his chin at Lord Sherbourne. "If you're the man in charge here, it's all the same to us." He cocked his head sharply back at Lady Sherbourne and said, "It might not matter *to whom* I'm speaking, neither. Dead people don't have no titles." He puffed himself up, threw out his chest. "I am charged to conduct a search of this house," he declared. His words were like the falling of an axe.

So it was as we feared. If Makepeace were found, Edward would die for sure. And a heretic's property was confiscate to the Queen. Kate and the girls would be penniless. I prayed that Kate would not be taken and executed too.

Similar thoughts must have gone on behind Kate's parents' eyes too, as well as considering their own fates. They stood their ground and did not reply to the man's declaration, although they were both as pale as ashes.

A mad thought sneaked into my head. What if I told them where he was? What if I did not make them search? Perhaps there would be mercy. Perhaps these men's masters would not blame Kate. They might even let her keep the property.

The man seemed pleased with the silence he had struck into his noble listeners. He looked around at his men again and smirked. I took a deep breath and readied myself. I opened my mouth to speak up.

"Enough of this," the man said. My voice died in my throat. "We have had a long ride and I want to find myself a bed. Where have you hidden it?"

Lord and Lady Sherbourne exchanged a glance. "I have no idea what you are talking about, man," he said. A slight tremor gave the lie to his words.

I steeled myself to try again. Come *on*, Molly – these men have kept at it for days in houses when they're sure. Weeks, even. Even if they have to take it apart stick by stick, they'll find the hole eventually.

"We know it's in the study. Where's that?"

Genuine surprise crossed Kate's parents' faces for a moment. Then they smoothed their expressions. It was a good thing nobody was taking any notice of me. My jaw might have been hanging on the floor.

"Come on – Sir Edward's study. We know that's where it's hidden."

Lord Sherbourne recovered quickest. With one eyebrow raised, he nodded into the gloom at the side of the hall where the door was closed on Edward's room.

Most of the men moved in that direction, except for two, including the leering one by my side, whose job it seemed to be to watch us.

"One moment," said Lord Sherbourne. He had regained the natural authority of his voice. "You have not told us your name, nor who your master is, nor what you are looking for." The leader of the search team turned back, his look openly insolent. He paused, seeming to consider his reply. Eventually, he said only, "You're quite right, milord. I didn't." Then he swept around on his heel and gestured to his men to follow.

It was odd for nobility to stand in the cold, dark hall while the men searched Edward's study, and yet the alternative was to have our guards follow us back to the parlour where Makepeace was hidden in the wall. No other room, save the bedchambers, had a fire lit. I saw Kate's parents' minds work on the problem in time with my own and waited helplessly for their decision.

Lady Sherbourne addressed the nearer of the men, saying, "If we are to be guarded, we *will* be guarded in comfort, at least. Whatever you fellows are looking for, you will not discover it easily, for there is nothing to find. You may follow us or not, as you please."

She and her husband returned to the parlour before the men could reply. The one Lady Sherbourne had spoken to followed, looking sheepish. The other, the one with filthy teeth, leered suggestively at me again and I attempted to copy Kate's mother's way of looking down at a taller person. His expression switched to looking put out. I wondered if he were used to women being flattered by his pungent attentions, though I doubted it. I determined not to look at him again. I followed them into the parlour, leaving him to guard the hall and door alone.

The wait in the parlour was short but painful. Lady Sherbourne took up Makepeace's seat at the chess table and moved some pieces around the board on her turns. I knew that she had never learned the game, declaring it a waste of time. Her husband tried to look as if he were considering her strategy, but once or twice he could not conceal his bafflement. At least the man guarding us was unlikely to know how to play or to suspect that she couldn't.

Kate stared into the fire, her needlework idle in her lap. She did not acknowledge the man who leaned against her wall in his dirty cloak. Jane continued her sewing or at least pretended to do so, but kept looking up at the man, at her distracted mother, or at me... anywhere, I think, to keep herself from looking at the place a few feet away where an illegal priest was hiding. I tried to let Jane know by my eyes that she should sit still but her astonishment – and probably fear – was too great.

It was hard for me, too, not to focus on that part of the panelling. Every moment, I knew with every fibre of my soul that something was going to give the game away. The men were going to burst in and declare they had made a mistake and they wanted to search this room instead. Or they would stay where they were for hours and hours, taking the place apart in vain, while Makepeace slowly suffocated in the priest hole.

When they found nothing, what then? When no hiding place came to light – *who had told them there was one, anyway?* – would they leave or would they widen their search? Would they question us? And how?

It was a small mercy that I did not torture myself with these thoughts for long. We had been in the parlour only minutes when heavy boots sounded in the passageway. Every pair of eyes turned fearfully to the door. Our guard stood upright from his slouched position against the wall, opened the door and stuck his head out.

The next moment, his master came in and took in the sight of Kate's parents, then Jane and finally Kate herself. His smile was triumphant.

"Lady Spicer," he said. "You would have done better to have burned this than hidden it. You might have saved your husband."

In his hand was a letter, the seal broken. It was Edward's seal.

CHAPTER THIRTEEN

Kate made a sound between a scream and a cry. Her hand flew to her mouth. For once, her mother had nothing to say.

"Yes, madam," said the man. "Your husband's letter. Not a good hiding place, behind books, even if we hadn't known where to look." This wasn't just a job to this man. He was enjoying himself. I felt fury rise in my chest.

"He will be arrested, madam, if he hasn't already been taken. This" – he waved Edward's letter – "this will see him burned. Or he might be let off with the axe, I suppose."

Arrested. Questioned. My mind flew from Edward to Ned, and the anger in me twisted into dread. Would they take Ned too? What would they do to him? Horrible images of Ned in pain flashed before my eyes, ending with a vision of fire. No kind axe for him. Would his letter to me prove his innocence? Would they take notice? I didn't know.

A moment later I was ashamed of my selfish thoughts, but there they were. I thought of the times I had scolded Ned, the times I had made him wait to marry me until we had put by enough money. And now it would not matter if I were heiress to a fortune.

Kate's shoulders heaved. Jane gripped the arms of her chair tightly and her eyes were glazed as she stared at this man holding her father's seal. Her grandmother clutched a chess piece and her mouth gaped, all her airs and graces forgotten. They were almost my own family. I might lose them as well as Ned.

Lord Sherbourne roused himself first. He stood and faced the man, who placed his hand on the hilt of his sword. "On what charge?" he said carefully.

"Why, heresy, milord. Of the worst type."

Heresy? My mind spun even faster. Not... preferring the company of men? Or was that heresy? If so, was it the *worst* type? I didn't know these answers either.

I could not see Lord Sherbourne's face, but I could see the man's as he held up the lost – stolen – letter like a trophy. Realisation crept in that Lord Sherbourne did not understand him and he tilted his head. His smile returned.

"I did not think that *I* would tell you." His eyes flicked to Kate and back again. She was sobbing quietly now in little gasps. "Although I think Lady Spicer already knows what her husband is."

He left room for a pause, relishing his torture. "Milord, your daughter's husband is an unbeliever. An atheist."

Kate's parents turned to look at her.

"Katherine," her mother said. "Kate..."

Kate shook her head vigorously, her hands still covering her face. "No," she said. "No... no."

I did not know whether she was denying the charge against her husband or denying her mother's enquiry.

Our situation shifted once again. The nature of the family I thought I served pivoted on its axis. I had heard of Catholics being arrested, fined, even executed. I was familiar with that danger. I had heard of men being punished for sodomy – those who were not quiet about it, at least – and I knew about the shame that was heaped on their families. But I had never heard of someone who did not *believe*. That was just made up for plays on the stage, I thought. There was sometimes a character dragged screaming by demons down to Hell at the end, disappearing into the bowels of the playhouse. Nobody would stand with Edward and fight his case. The risk would be too great. My thoughts flew back to Ned. Would he be dragged down screaming too?

Lord Sherbourne drew himself upright once more, though it looked like it took all his willpower.

"Ridiculous," he said. "Better men than you will have to prove that."

"That's as may be." The man shrugged. He looked past Lord Sherbourne at Kate. "Did you answer the letter, madam?" he asked. "I wonder if it is among the papers we found at your husband's inn in London? Or whether it will be on his person when he is found?"

Their lodgings had been searched. This new information silenced the room. Edward was a wanted man. And what of Ned? Kate's man was in danger – and what of mine?

He unfolded the letter and held it at an angle to catch enough light. He scanned to find the words he wanted, making as much display as he could, enjoying his power.

"I wonder how you replied to this line, for instance," he said. He read aloud:

My dearest wife, I have been persuaded by many and

*diverse arguments not only of the opinions that I have
shared with you already, but also that Religion itself is
false. It has been made clear to me that a beginning to
Religion was only made by men to keep their fellow men
in fear.*

The silence in which we sat or stood before was nothing to
the dumbfounded stupor that engulfed us now.

The man looked at Kate's father, her mother and Kate
herself in turn, defying their right of nobility to correct his
behaviour. Still with his eyes on Kate, he folded the letter and
placed it inside his shirt. "These few words are enough to
condemn him, madam. Have no doubt of that."

Kate's face ran with tears. She made no attempt to stop their
flow.

Dimly, I understood that the men were leaving now they
had what they had come for. I was numb as I followed them
from the parlour back to the hall, where they all gathered again
as a group. A lifetime of habit made me go to the door and open
it for them.

In the doorway stood Edward. Behind him, holding their
exhausted horses, was Ned.

Edward took the men by surprise. He burst into the hall and
through it towards the parlour, shouting for Kate. It was several
moments before they followed, drawing their weapons. Every
one of them went – nobody thought to see if Edward had arrived
alone.

I slipped outside, pulled the door almost closed behind me,
and flung myself into Ned's arms.

"You mustn't be seen," I said. "They will take you too, I know they will."

"How long have they been here?"

There was distant shouting from inside the house. "Long enough. They have found the letter. You must go. You mustn't let them see you."

His jaw set hard. "I am not a coward, Molly."

I took a deep breath. Men and their *good names*. I wanted to scream. Instead, I said in Ned's ear, "I know you are not. But what use will you be to me, or to him, or to anyone, if you are arrested as well? You won't even be able to tell the family what's happened. They need you here." I paused. "*I* need you here."

Ned held me at arm's length. He glared at me. A terrible twisting seized my gut. His bloody pride would kill him.

A bobbing lantern caught my eye from where the men's horses were drinking at the water trough. I took a sharp breath. It came closer and I saw it was Old Ned. I let the breath go again. The raised voices were travelling inside the house, coming back this way. As well as voices came the ring of steel on steel.

Old Ned reached us and I appealed to him. "Make him go," I said, gesturing to Ned. I was beginning to panic. "Make him hide. They're arresting Sir Edward – they'll take him too."

He looked from me to Ned and back again. Ned quickly summed up what was happening and what sort of men Edward had been meeting in London. His father's eyes grew round.

"Molly is right," Old Ned said. "They'll take you too. They'll get information out of you. You might think you'll keep quiet – but they will get what they want in the end."

"Please hide, Ned. I won't let you be taken. When I am your wife, you will be in charge. But right now, do as I say. Hide with the horses and then come in through the kitchens."

He wouldn't budge. "Moll, they must know he's got a man with him. He wouldn't travel alone. I'm not having them drag me out of the hayloft," said Ned.

In desperation, I turned back to Ned's father.

"Give me your cloak," he said. Ned and I gawped at him. "Maybe they know he's got a man called Ned with him. So that's me. But there's a difference between doing things to a young 'un like you and doing them to a deaf old man, especially one who's maybe going a bit daft into the bargain... a bit too daft to remember what he's seen."

I grasped at this idea and looked eagerly at Ned. It occurred to me that his father hadn't misheard a single word we had said, even though we were hissing in quick undertones. Ned still looked sullen but didn't speak.

"I mean it, son. Give me your cloak and go. This'll be the most use I've been in years."

He was still going to refuse. "I need you, Ned," I said. "I need you whole, and healthy, and here with me."

Reluctantly, he pulled off his travelling cloak and passed it to his father.

I slipped back inside the hall. There was too much happening for anyone to notice. Edward was not making it easy for them. He had lost his sword and hat in the skirmish and was swearing fit to raise a devil. Spittle flew along with his curses.

They had to tear Kate away from him. She had come with them, clutching at his cloak. Jane followed behind, clinging to her grandfather as the men wrestled her father's arms behind his back. It was a degrading spectacle, yet I was glad that it gave Ned's father a few precious moments to get into position.

"Where are you taking him?" said Kate between sobs, latching herself onto the arm of the leader.

"Madam, you shouldn't care," he said, and attempted to disengage himself.

"He is my husband. You must tell me."

Perhaps the man felt some pity or perhaps he just wanted to make her let go of him, but he said, "Tonight we will keep him ourselves. Tomorrow, we will take him to the gaol in Rysham. Seek him there."

Kate loosened her grip on his sleeve and he shook himself free. She stood back, her face as pale as death. Edward was still struggling for his freedom against the three men who held him. A fourth came towards him with a length of rope and made to tie his hands behind his back.

It was Jane who stepped forward then and picked up her father's hat from the floor. She walked around the men to Edward. One of them moved to block her path. To my surprise – and I think to the man's surprise – she did not back down. She held his gaze for several beats until he stood aside. She stood directly in front of Edward and said, "Father."

The whole hall became still. The man with the rope stopped mid-knot. Edward stopped struggling and looked at his daughter, become a woman in his absence. The frenzy left his face. His shoulders slumped, defeated.

She stood straight and tall. In a firm voice she said, "Your hat, sir." Then she dropped a perfect curtsey and came back up to look him in the face again.

Still nobody moved. Slowly, Edward rolled back his shoulders and lifted his head. Feeling the difference in him, the men shared quick glances, then stepped away from him, removing the rope. I saw now that Edward was taller than every one of these men by at least half a head. He took his hat from Jane, brushed the dust from it, and placed it carefully on his head.

"I thank you, madam," he said, simply.

He took Jane by the shoulders and kissed her white cheek. Then he looked around himself to seek the most senior of the men.

The one in charge stepped forward, paused, then bowed as if he were compelled to rather than wished to. "Sir Edward Spicer, you are arrested. Come with us."

Edward inclined his head as if accepting an invitation. He turned to Kate, bowed formally, and went away with them into the night.

CHAPTER FOURTEEN

We stood in the hall long after the bobbing lights had disappeared. I felt anxious for Old Ned, but surely they would not mistreat an old man. I hoped he was right about that.

I approached Kate's father to tell him about the switched places. "Ned might shed some light on all this, my lord," I said. "Shall I find him?"

He nodded and I scurried off to the kitchens. I found Ned being plied with pottage by Cook. The gaggle of servants who had crept into the hall when the men came knocking were now lurking here. Everyone tried to look busy but stayed within earshot. I pursed my lips at them, though it had no effect down here. The kitchens were Cook's domain.

"You're wanted," I said. The less said for this gawping audience, the better.

He put down his spoon and followed me back. I wondered what sort of story he had to tell.

Lord Sherbourne had released Makepeace. With everything that had just happened, I had forgotten about him. I clenched my teeth and wished everyone else had forgotten about Make-peace too. Those men knew what they were looking for and where it was hidden. There was only one person who could have told them.

Makepeace had not passed out this time, more's the pity. He was sat at the table laid for chess and helping himself to a mug of ale. Of course, he had written precise instructions to lead them to Edward's letter. He had made sure he wouldn't suffer much, no matter how much he made everyone else suffer.

I was beginning to piece it together. A couple of days ago when he went missing, he was finding a messenger to tell someone about Edward's letter to Kate. That was why he came home so happy, I would have sworn to it. I felt sick when it occurred to me that the paper he had dripped his poison onto, and the pen and ink he had used, were the ones I had helpfully brought him from Kate's own writing desk. The nauseous sensa-tion became a pounding in my ears as my blood boiled.

He abused the hospitality and protection of the family he had singlehandedly thrown into disaster. I began to shake at the knees with rage. I only held my silence because I knew he was about to be exposed – unless he would find a way to twist things and blame me.

Lord Sherbourne had aged years within that hour. Deep shadows etched his face. Lady Sherbourne looked weary and thin, though she sat rigidly next to the fire. Jane held her moth-er's hand in both of hers and stroked it with her thumb.

Ned stood and waited to be questioned and I hung by his side. Eventually, Kate's father puffed out a deep breath. I gripped Ned's arm as if even death would never peel me away. Makepeace wasn't about to confess his part in this evening's disaster. He would blame someone else – me, Ned maybe. I would have to speak up when he did. I knew my word against him would count for nothing yet I had to try. I couldn't leave while he spewed his poison.

I breathed hard as I looked around at the faces – Kate's and her mother's distraught ones, her father's beaten one, Jane's concerned, motherly one, and then that of Makepeace, which was oddly serene.

Lord Sherbourne saved me from making a mutiny. "You might as well stay, Molly," he said. His voice was an old man's tremor, his humour turned sour as week-old cream. "You'll hear it all soon enough anyway." He jerked his head at Ned and made a snort of acknowledging the obvious. I bobbed my thanks at him, then I let go of Ned. He gave me a gentle push to go and sit on my stool behind Kate's shoulder.

"Well, Ned?" said Lord Sherbourne. "Tell us everything you know."

As I had guessed, a letter had been sent to London.

They hadn't spent the night in *The Swan* but in another part of the city, with Edward's friends. The talking and drinking had continued until late and nobody in their right mind would go about London at that hour. In the morning, Ned had been sent to the inn ahead of Edward to order breakfast.

One of *The Swan's* servants stopped him at the back door and warned him to leave. Men had arrived during the night and searched their rooms; they were waiting to arrest them.

Ned did the only thing possible. He hurried back to the house where Edward was mounting his horse. He gave him the news and the two of them left London that instant. Edward's friends fled too. Ned didn't know where. I didn't care.

They would have made it home sooner, before the men who searched the study, even, had not Edward's horse thrown a shoe. A blacksmith can only work so fast, even if you *do* pay him double.

The servants at *The Swan* had heard frightening words from the gossipy men who were waiting for Edward to return. They frightened me when Ned repeated them. The threat of being called a heretic was nothing new. We had lived with that word for years. But much rarer words were muttered too. Apostasy. Atheism. There was no saving Edward from that. He was ruined – not only were his reputation and his fortune forfeit, but his life. I looked towards Kate, still clutching Jane's hand. This spelled disaster for them too.

There wasn't much more that Ned could say, except that the men lying in wait to seize Edward for their bounty had boasted that even if the pamphlets they had found in the best rooms of *The Swan* weren't enough to kill a man, the words written in Edward's own hand and hidden in his study at home certainly would be. They knew where it was because a letter had told them where to look.

"Sir Edward wanted to get back here fast," Ned said. "He knew what letter they meant and we had to get here first and burn it." Ned looked at Kate, raising his hands in apology. "We rode hard, madam, but not hard enough."

I had never heard Ned say so many words in one go. He had never had so many important words to say. There was silence. Every face was grave, though I was sure a sneer was pulling at Makepeace's upper lip. I clenched my fists in the folds of my skirts, digging my nails into my palms until it hurt. Inwardly I screamed *It was him! He did it!*

Why could they not see it? Who else could have written a

letter to London? Who else *would* have done it? I longed to slap his face, to claw at his eyes, to strip away the mask and let everyone see him for what he was. I sat still, my teeth clenched.

Lord Sherbourne spoke finally. "This letter, Ned. I suppose it was unsigned."

"I believe so, my Lord. Delivered to a bishop in London and passed on."

Kate's father nodded. "And the hand that wrote it also stole *your* letter, Kate. We can assume that much."

Makepeace looked about himself and then pointedly at me. He cleared his throat and raised his eyebrows, sat back in his chair and crossed his arms over his chest. I felt myself colouring under all the eyes which moved to look at me. However, he must do better than that to pin the blame on me.

Kate intervened. "Not Molly, Father. It couldn't have been her. She does not write."

The priest's swaggering air faltered. "But you have taught her, have you not, madam? Your husband insists on educating his servants."

"She reads. But writes... no. Certainly no more than her name, and that in plain letters."

"Ah," he said. "Ah, I think I understand, Lady Spicer." He sat back again, relaxed and self-assured.

It was Kate's turn to look uncertain.

Her father thumped the table suddenly, making everyone but Makepeace jump. "Well, I wish *I* understood it. Enlighten me, Father, for God's sake."

Makepeace seemed willing to ignore his blasphemy, only momentarily raising an eyebrow.

"Of course, my Lord," Makepeace said. His voice was smooth, oily even. "It is so obvious now. I only wish I had realised before. The current sad situation might have been avoided." He smiled his slow, deliberate smile, enjoying the moment.

"The only possible answer, sir, is that Lady Spicer sent the letter herself."

The room stared at him in stunned silence. Lord Sherbourne was lost for words and Makepeace watched him try to comprehend the new idea. The corners of his mouth turned upwards ever so slightly. He could not help himself.

Before Kate's father or mother could find the words they wanted to say – and certainly before Kate could defend herself – Makepeace continued speaking. "It explains, madam," he said, nodding deferentially at Lady Sherbourne, whose eyebrows were raised arches, "why your daughter would not take your excellent advice and turn Molly out of the house when the letter went missing. Perhaps I was mistaken when I saw Molly put a letter in her pocket. Or perhaps..." He stroked his chin, looking meaningfully at Kate, then me, then Kate again, and back to Lady Sherbourne. "No... it is not my place to wonder such things."

He dipped his head in a show of humility. I watched his meaning occur to Lady Sherbourne. Her eyebrows raised even higher and her mouth fell open. Jerkily she turned to study Kate, looking at her as if she had shed her skin and sat there in the form of a snake.

"No," she said. "No, no. Kate, tell me you didn't." Lady Sherbourne shook her head violently. "Your own husband! What he wrote was awful, but Father Makepeace could have saved him, could have brought him back to the truth. And Edward behaved badly, I know... but –"

"No! You think *I* wrote to London? And I made Molly part

of it? How could you think that? I love him," said Kate. She stood quickly, her cheeks reddened and her breath coming hard.

"But you did write a letter," her father said. His voice was low and quavering. He too looked at Kate as if she was a stranger. "And you sent it with Edward's messenger."

"Yes," she said, "a letter to Edward."

There was silence again. A disbelieving silence. This was spiralling out of control. Out of Kate's control – I had never had any power in the first place. I wondered how long the priest had spent planning this. I wanted to stand up and scream, to shout how he had done it all and was twisting every fact out of all its truth. But I could not. My belly seemed to have turned to water.

Makepeace eventually spoke. When he did, he was measured and deliberate. "I beg your pardon, madam, but how do we – I mean – how does your father know that you wrote to your husband?"

Ned coughed. I had forgotten that he was there. "My Lord," he said. Lord Sherbourne also appeared surprised at Ned's being there. Ned continued, in his slow, sure voice, "A letter arrived for Sir Edward yesterday. I took it from the messenger myself. The cover was in my lady's hand. I would swear to that."

I could have kissed him. Makepeace threw a look of chagrin at Ned that made me suddenly fear for him. I did not want Ned to attract the man's revenge as well.

Makepeace was not done. "And was this messenger well known to you or to Sir Edward?" he asked Ned, managing to look down his broken nose at him from his seated position.

"No, Father," Ned admitted.

"So you wouldn't describe this man as a trusted friend?" Ned slowly shook his head. "Two letters, then," Makepeace said to Lord Sherbourne. "The second to the bishop. And a well-paid messenger."

I thought back to that day. Kate had taken her letter to the messenger herself rather than through me. Had she sent a second letter? Would she? My first reaction was no. Kate loved Edward. But she had been jittery for days, ever since receiving his letter. Had she been expecting a search party? Had she hidden the letter for them to find and claimed it was stolen?

Eyes slid sideways to Kate – I watched every pair of them from under my eyelashes. They all asked the same silent questions as I asked. My own eyes flickered towards her too. I was immediately ashamed of my doubts when I saw her wide eyes and open, speechless mouth. Makepeace was the one to watch, I told myself. I flicked my eyes back towards him.

While everyone else observed Kate's shocked face and no doubt made their minds up whether she was innocent or guilty, he met my eyes. Unwatched by anyone else, the devil behind his gaze smirked out at me.

Next morning, Old Ned arrived with a letter for Kate from Edward. He was pale and tired but had not been harmed. I gave a fervent prayer of thanks for that.

I was tired myself after a night dreaming of ravens and devils, but I knew that I would have slept far worse had my own Ned been taken with Edward. They would have treated him differently from his father. I shuddered to think of what they might have done to him. I took the letter Old Ned held out to me and a wave of gratitude and affection flowed over me. It struck me that he was the closest to a father I had known in many years.

I put my arms on his shoulders and kissed his cheek. After a moment, he patted my back. I stepped back and he gave me a toothless smile. "They asked me a few questions, but I couldn't answer them. They'll all leave me be and let me come and go, I think. It sometimes pays to be a deaf and daft old man, Molly," he said with a wink, and I laughed through my tears. He touched my elbow and lowered his voice. "I left Sir Edward under lock and key in the village inn, but they're taking him into Rysham and leaving him in their gaol. The Lent Assizes are happening. I am to fetch a few things and go there too. It's my guess they're afraid he'll escape if they take him all the way to London. Or they get their bounty either way. That's all I know."

He gave another smile, a sad one this time, and hobbled off, saddle-sore, towards the kitchens. Cook would feed him well. Everyone there would know what had happened by now. Everyone loved Ned, and now they would love his father too.

The smile died on my lips when I looked at the letter in my hand. The paper was small and poor, the best available at the village inn. It was unsealed, of course. No privacy for a prisoner.

Kate's name was shakily written. I wondered what they had done to Edward already, and what the gaolers at Rysham would do. I did not think a little gaol would have the terrible machines I had heard of in London, those they kept in the Tower, but they would have simple means of getting people to talk. Everyone had heard stories. I shook my head to rid my imagination of such things. They wouldn't be doing that, surely. Not to Edward. He was a knight, not a common man.

I put the letter in my pocket and hurried inside.

Kate was still in bed. I took her some fresh bread along with the letter. She was tangled in her sheets between sleep and wakefulness when I went in. Her night had been as troubled as mine, and no surprise. I opened the curtains so she could see I had brought something important for her.

She became alert quickly, sitting upright and holding out her hand. I gave her the letter and she tore it open. I moved away to a discreet distance and began spreading butter on her bread, all the while sneaking looks at her. She read greedily. It must have been short because she very soon let the paper fall onto the bed.

I held my tongue and waited for an order. I began to think Kate had forgotten I was there but she spoke eventually. Her eyes were dry and her voice was low and calm.

"He did it, didn't he, Molly?"

I was confused.

Kate looked up at me. "Makepeace," she said. I noticed she had dropped the title from his name. I nodded.

"I ought to have believed you. Of course you wouldn't steal a letter. It was him," Kate said. "He stole it and wrote a letter of his own to London. He has killed my husband."

My tongue would not move. I nodded again.

"And now he accuses both you and me."

I nodded again. Kate was so poised, so controlled, so... different. It made me tongue-tied. I had expected to be offering her comfort, if she would accept it, but she was flat calm.

"Do you know what his letter to me says, Molly?"

At first, I thought she was accusing me of prying into this second letter and I began to protest.

"No, no, Molly," she said, seeing the hurt and alarm on my face. "I do not mean that. I mean I want to tell you what he says."

She paused for me to understand. I stopped protesting and listened.

"He says that he will refuse to plead."

CHAPTER FIFTEEN

I hadn't expected that. I must have looked stupidly at Kate.

"He won't answer the charge against him," she said. "When the justice asks him if he is innocent or guilty, he says he will not answer. If he does not plead, the trial cannot happen."

My heart leapt for a moment. Did that mean he could walk free? Kate's serious face gave me my answer. *Of course not.* If that were true, every criminal would refuse to answer their charge.

She explained it patiently. "They will press him to death, Molly. That is the punishment for refusing to plead. They will put him under wooden boards and weigh him down until he answers or until he dies."

Kate's face was set in hard lines. She looked nothing like herself. The softness was gone and her mother looked out from her eyes.

So either way, he would die. The axe – which had some honour and might be swift – or the indignity of being crushed. But why choose the latter? My brow creased, then the answer hit me in the gut. He was saving Kate. He was saving her twice over. I wondered if she realised it.

"That man has done it," she said. This time I knew who she meant. "He has killed my husband," she said again. "He could have counselled him, talked him around, brought him back. He could have comforted him when we lost Harry. He could have been patient, forgiven him. But he didn't do any of those things. He took revenge instead. He wrote a letter like a coward and blamed me – and blamed you too. He is not a man of God. He is a devil. I should have seen it before. Perhaps we could have done something. I am sorry, Molly. For everything. I hope you can forgive me."

Kate gazed at me. *She* was asking *my* forgiveness, and I did not know where to put myself. I was suddenly aware of everything about myself – how I was standing, the way my cheeks had flushed. I mumbled something, I hardly know what.

"You were curious about the letter, I know," Kate said, seeing my embarrassment. "But I can forgive that if you can forgive me." She held out her hand to me and I took it, and she placed her other hand on top. "I need you, Molly. We know what he is and he will destroy us for that if we do not stop him. Or else he will keep us waiting. We will be at his mercy."

"But how do we stop him?" I asked.

Kate paused and drooped her head. "I don't know," she said. She released my hand, gesturing for me to sit next to her bed. I perched on the edge. My mind began working harder than it ever had. Kate needed me. I would do anything for her. Not just as a maid. As a friend. Almost – did I dare even think it? – as a sister.

"This has changed everything, Molly," Kate said. She spoke softly, leaning towards me, and I leaned in towards her too.

"*Everything.* I knew Edward was not very religious. He never spent much time at prayer but it never concerned me much. I felt safe – he would never attract attention and end up a martyr." She laughed breathily and her lip curled. "I never imagined this."

Me too, I longed to say. Everything had changed for me too. Life's certainties had crumbled. How could it be that a priest will lie to protect himself, yet a non-believer will choose a bad death for others' sake?

"I wonder how long he has doubted," she continued. "Years, I suspect, but losing Harry... He said in that letter, the one from London, that a God who takes a child such as Harry is *no God of his.*" She whispered the last words and looked around her, although we were quite alone. Her hand went to her mouth, ashamed of what it had said.

I shifted on the chair. When we lost Harry, I had been comforted to know that he was in a better place, while Edward had tortured himself with these dark thoughts. I'd had no idea. No wonder he had behaved as he did with those devils on his back. Kate was right. Makepeace should have helped. He had cast him off, condemned and destroyed him and now he would seek to destroy us too.

I remembered another bedroom, where Kate sat in another bed. The pox marks on her hands were still fresh and frightening and Makepeace told her they were signs of her sinful nature and that her beloved sister was dead. I had not really looked at her hands in years. The scars on them had become merely part of Kate. Makepeace and his coldness had also become part of life. I had known he was there but was no longer shocked by him. We had lived with his ugly nature for so long that I was blind to it. But no more.

Kate was right. Makepeace was a devil in disguise. We had harboured him all these years and now he would torment us forever, or destroy us, if we did not stop him first. I knew she would never think of a way. She was not capable of it. However, an idea was making its way into my mind. It was a horrible idea, which is why I had it, not Kate.

Yet I could not do this thing alone. I needed her as much as she needed me. I would do it. I would bear the burden of it as much as I could. The thought made my knees shake, but not because I feared I could not do it. I knew I *was* capable and that knowledge was terrifying. I appalled myself. And I had to play a part to Kate in order to bring it about. I steeled myself to the task and smoothed my face.

Kate had picked up her note from Edward again but stared blankly at it. She had fallen into her own reverie. I coughed gently and she came back to the present moment. I picked my way through what I wanted to say. I remembered Old Ned's words when he gave me that note. *It pays to be deaf and daft.* I also thought of what my mother always said when I spoke too quickly – and too stupidly, I realised now. *Ask a question, Molly. Questions are safer.* Very well. I would combine those two lessons. I would ask a daft question and feel my way from there.

"Why does your husband not plead innocent? One letter cannot condemn a man, can it? And a letter written in grief, too. Or he could confess, but also talk to a priest who could help him – even one of the new ones – and he could promise not to doubt again."

Kate smiled sadly at me and patted my hand as if I were a simpleton.

"There were other papers found in London, remember. If it were any other charge, Edward or my father might be able to carry their influence, but not against this. Besides, you do not know why he will not plead."

I held my breath. I knew the answer, but I needed Kate to say it.

"He knows he cannot escape death. But if he pleads guilty or is found guilty – which he would be –the girls and I will penniless. I will have to throw us all onto my father's goodwill, and after his death onto my brother's. We will have nothing. As if I care about that!"

Bless her. That was only a part of it. She hadn't realised the extent of what Edward's sacrifice meant. He was saving them from a lot more than reliance on her brother – and a life under the same roof as her brother's wife.

Kate went on, her voice beginning to quaver. "They would not burn him – probably. He would go to the block. That would be less awful." Her mouth trembled. She began to gasp as she said, "But I know he will never give them an answer. He will be crushed. Doesn't he know I don't care about the house or the money! I am going to him tomorrow, Molly. I will make them let me see him so I can tell him so. I won't let him do it just so we can keep this!" She threw her arms up to indicate the roof under which we slept.

"I wonder, madam," I said, picking my way through a sentence, "I wonder whether your husband is saving you – and maybe others, perhaps Ned, even Jane – from a worse fate than poverty." Kate furrowed her brow at me. "I may be wrong," I added quickly. "I am sure your father will know... but when they try someone, do they not also *question* others who might have information?"

Kate's face lost its colour. I continued, "If a trial does not begin – perhaps that means they cannot do that. It would begin and end with him alone. I think he is doing it to protect you."

Kate showed her father the letter as soon as she was dressed. It was a fine spring day and she came to find me afterwards while I was spreading laundry over the bushes. She led me into the garden where we could not be overheard.

"You were right," she said as soon as we were out of earshot of the house. I bit my lip. I had to tread carefully. "Edward is protecting us, just as you said. My father said that he doubted he could influence the trial if Edward pleaded innocent, and it looks as though he is choosing the worse death to be kind to me. Molly, I cannot bear this."

"Your husband is brave, madam. And selfless."

She nodded. I spoke my next words very, very slowly. And quietly, in her ear. One misstep would spell a fresh disaster.

"Do you think we might hope the Almighty will take pity on him for that? Perhaps he is not so damned as we think?"

I breathed carefully and waited, watching Kate's face. I was sure these words were heresy. Yet a Heaven that agreed with our cowardly, devilish priest and cast a loving father and husband into the pit felt... impossible.

"But Father Makepeace, Molly, he would say..." and her words gave out. I nodded. She gazed at me, understanding growing in her eyes.

"Yes, madam, he would. But you said it yourself. He is a devil. We cannot trust his word. On anything. He knows we know what he is. And we must stop him before he finds a way to destroy us. Because he will."

Kate frowned, doubting. I had to press the point further, no matter how guilty I felt for it. "And what will become of Jane? Isabel?" I said.

Kate looked startled. "What of them? What can he do to them?"

"If Makepeace convinces your father that you – or you and I together – sent a letter that betrayed your husband, might he not take the girls from you? Who knows what poison Makepeace might then feed your daughters, without you to shield them."

I had appalled myself before but now I truly sickened myself. "You have lost a husband and one child already, madam. Please do not allow him to take the others."

Kate's hand reached up to her cheek as though I had slapped her. I was no less cruel than Makepeace but I was now so far mired in this business that I must go through and not turn back. It was for the best.

I forced myself to look Kate steadily in the eye. If I looked away in shame, it would be over. I could almost see the thoughts as they filed through her mind. Grief. Fear. Anger. Guilt. Finally, determination.

"To save my girls," she said, "I would do anything. I could not save Harry and I cannot save my husband but I must save the girls. What do you think we should do?"

Cautiously, I gave Kate the idea of my plan. In hushed voices, we discussed how and when we would put it into motion.

At dinner, Kate announced her intentions to give the servants notice and to close up her house.

"I cannot stay here," she said. "There are too many memories. I must go to Rysham and see Edward. If he really cannot be saved, I shall bring him home for burial and place him next to

Harry. Then I shall go. Jane, Isabel and I shall find another home."

Makepeace looked up from his meal and stared hard at Kate. At his elbow, Lady Sherbourne said, "Where can you go without this following you?" She held up her hand to prevent Kate from answering. "I understand that you want to leave here, Katherine. That is very well. But come home to your father's house. You can live quietly. We can keep you away from people's gossip. We can help you. We can all help you," she said, glancing towards her husband and then towards Makepeace.

I could scarcely believe that Lady Sherbourne could be so blind as to believe Kate had written to London. That man still controlled her.

Kate sat very still for several heartbeats. "Thank you, Mother," she said finally, "but I think we must find our own home." Lady Sherbourne began to protest but Kate said, "I shall be a widow. I am resigned to that. But I shall be an independent widow, thanks to my husband's courage."

Makepeace's expression stiffened and he made a *harrumph*. Kate did not deign to acknowledge him. I wished I could applaud her.

"However, I would be grateful to stay at your house for a short while, Father, until I have found us a suitable home. I mean to leave here as soon as possible after... after what must happen has happened."

Lord Sherbourne nodded. "If that is what you really want, Kate. But stay with us for a while and you may change your mind."

Kate agreed cautiously. She made no promises.

"I will go to Rysham tomorrow and stay until it is over. Molly and Ned will come with me. Mother, I would be grateful if you would oversee the house so we may leave when I have brought Edward home. As soon as possible."

Lady Sherbourne agreed, clearly impressed with Kate's new decisiveness.

"I shall come with you," said her father. "You do not have to do this alone."

She stuck out her chin. "I shall not be alone, Father."

He cast a dismissive glance in my direction. "You know my meaning, Kate. And I might be able to do something. Perhaps all is not lost. I can talk with the justice... manage things somehow. Arrange for clemency. There is nothing for me to do here. Your mother knows how to instruct maids, not I."

There was no disputing that. Kate thanked him, although there was no hope in her eyes. Makepeace said nothing, but a small smile of satisfaction crept onto his lips. I wondered what had pleased him.

CHAPTER SIXTEEN

We left for Rysham at daybreak and made good time. We entered the streets and the people parted for a lord and lady, but the glances were not the simple curiosity of common folk. People whispered behind hands, darted into shops and dwellings, and even stared outright. The identities of the prisoners were never a secret and word of a gentleman being held for trial had travelled fast. Ned sat tall in his saddle, keeping his head high. I shifted uneasily at his side and avoided eye contact with them. I was glad that Kate's father had accompanied her. Their behaviour may have been far worse without him.

In one of the better streets, a familiar figure stepped outside his door. Doctor Phillips was too slow to pretend he hadn't seen us. His good manners won out and he removed his hat, though he bowed awkwardly and stared at the dirt when he came up. The gossip had spread further than the servants and trades-people of the town, then. My heart hurt for Kate. I could only see the back of her head. She nodded an acknowledgement at Phillips then turned back to the road and kept her head high.

The assize justice heard cases in the Guildhall and so there we went. The justice was at his breakfast, Lord Sherbourne was told. A minute later, he and Kate were bowed into a private room, and Ned and I had waited in the main hall. It was busy with lawyers and clerks – I supposed – at tables littered with scrolls and books, various plaintiffs and defendants and family members – impossible to tell who was who – and the jurymen, stretching their legs after the early session.

We found a quieter corner with a view of the justice's quarters.

"I hoped to be married to you by now, Moll," Ned said.

"I know," I said. "You still want to? I mean, nothing's changed because of... all this?"

"As if it would, love," he said, giving me my favourite smile. "It would take a lot more than this to make me not want to marry you. Besides, I'd have thought it would be you changing your mind. It's the master who's accused, not the mistress. I've been with him all our lives."

His face remained strong, as always, but his voice gave away his worry. For the first time I thought of it from Ned's perspective. Some wife I would make, thinking of my husband only after everybody else. He must be grieving as much as anyone. And he really thought *I* might want to throw *him* off.

I took his hand and looked up into his face. "Ned Foster, I want to be your wife more than ever," I said. "You won't be rid of me that easily."

"I am glad to hear it," said a voice at Ned's elbow. Old Ned. A welcome face. Not for the first time, I wondered just how deaf Ned's father actually was.

My Ned and his father shook hands. "You've arrived none

too soon," Old Ned said. "I'm here just ahead of the master. He's next before the justice."

Sure enough, a commotion of raised voices and catcalling began outside. The hall grew silent to listen. The door where Kate had been ushered opened and out came a younger man than I had expected in black robes and cap. Behind him came Kate and her father, she visibly shaking and he grim-faced.

Under the arch into the hall came Edward, hands bound. He was pale, tired-looking and a little dirty, but seemingly unhurt.

"Edward," called Kate, and he turned to see her. He smiled as if his troubles had vanished in that instant. She tried to smile back.

A clerk called the court to order. The whole room knew by now who was next before the justice, and from the nudges and nods in her direction, everyone also knew who Kate was.

Ned, his father and I stayed in our corner at the back. Somebody placed stools at the side of the hall for Kate and her father. Edward stood alone in the expanse of floor before the justice's chair.

He spoke clearly to confirm his name. A ripple of murmurs went around the room. Then the justice said, "Sir Edward Spicer, you are accused of apostasy: namely, the crime of denying the authority of God. How do you plead?"

The entire hall held its breath. My hand crept into Ned's. I could not take my eyes off the face of the justice. He watched Edward without blinking, his face lean and serious.

When Edward spoke again it was in few words. "I neither confess nor do I swear my innocence. I refuse this trial."

Another ripple of muttering and gasps travelled the hall,

growing into shouts of, "Shame!" Several men got to their feet. Clerks and orderlies stepped forwards, holding their palms outwards to the public, placating them. The pair of soldiers at the archway looked nervous. Ned tensed at my side and gripped my hand.

Two more soldiers came into the hall and stood facing the public benches. The men settled back onto them, grumbling, and the justice could be heard.

"Sir Edward," he said, "you must plead either guilty or innocent, or be condemned."

Edward answered immediately, "I will not, sir."

The justice raised a warning finger to the men on the benches and their complaints merely rumbled. "This is the final time I shall ask," he said. "Are you guilty or innocent?"

Edward paused and looked over at Kate. She was frozen except for her hands, which were busy twisting her wedding ring around and around. He saw the familiar gesture and gave her a longing look. With his eyes on Kate, he said simply, "I shall not answer."

The justice sighed. "Then you leave me no choice. I sentence you to death, to be carried out by the town constables at the earliest opportunity, by the pressing of your body under great weights. This is at the pleasure and in the name of her glorious majesty, Elizabeth, Queen of England and Ireland.

And with that, Edward's court appearance was over. Two soldiers, at a nod from the justice, stepped one either side of him to escort him from the Guildhall to await his death. I was unsure whether their duty was to prevent an escape or to protect him from the mob who might anticipate the law.

Edward walked between them, exhausted but carrying himself proudly. He paused to speak low into Kate's ear, then took her hand – the one on which she wore his wedding ring – in his bound hands and bent over it to kiss it.

Then he was gone.

Kate visited him later that day, taking him a clean shirt. Old Ned had worked himself in well with the gaolers with his deaf simpleton act and only a small bribe was necessary to allow Kate and Edward some time alone.

The gaol was not the hellish pit I had imagined. Not like the London gaols I had heard of, and I gave thanks for that small mercy. He was in the best room in the house, too, and had it to himself. I had seen worse quarters in some roadside inns, although they had no bars at the windows.

The greeting between us all was sombre. Edward shook hands with Kate's father, Ned, and even with me before he and Kate were left alone. Then we waited in strained silence in the small constables' room for Kate to knock and be let out of Edward's room.

Old Ned had been staying at *The White Hart* close by the gaol and he had taken more rooms for us. Kate did not speak on our walk there. When we arrived she spent some time talking privately with Lord Sherbourne, and I had some precious time with Ned at the fireplace. We did not talk much. Every conversation only led back to what was happening. We sat in companionable quiet, ignoring the sidelong looks of the townsfolk also supping there.

I served supper for Kate and her father. Ned came along, although it did not take more than one person to serve two, especially since neither had much appetite. They did not comment on it except to say they were glad we were together again.

"In fact, very soon you need never be apart again," Kate said. "My husband told me that he wishes you to be married as soon as may be. As soon as we get home. He hoped for a day of joy for us after the sadness."

I did not know what to say so said nothing. This was all I had wanted for myself for so long. Yet at this time... I looked up at Ned. He felt the same way.

Kate saw our faces and said, "I know it seems strange. But he was adamant. He will feel a small degree of peace to know you will not wait any longer. He knows you would have married in the winter if he had not taken Ned to London. And I wish it too," she said, tears forming again. "Happiness can be taken from us at any moment. You should not wait."

Lord Sherbourne made a noise in his throat to show his agreement. His eyes glistened and he turned his head away.

Ned took my hand in both of his and kissed it. Kate cried and smiled at the same time. I had no heart to argue.

In the morning, Old Ned arrived with news. He muttered to me and Ned that Edward's death was arranged for two days' time. It would be Good Friday.

Ned sat heavily on the bench at the fireplace and put his head in his hands. I laid a hand on his shoulder. It became real at that moment for me, and perhaps only then for Ned too. The hearing in the Guildhall was playacting. Edward's arrest a few days ago was a dream. Edward was alive and well. How was it possible he would be dead so soon?

"Someone must tell the mistress," Old Ned said.

The someone had to be me. My guts roiled at it but it had to be done immediately and so I went to find Kate. She was with her father in their small private sitting room. I was relieved they were not in a public part of the inn.

"What is it?" she said. My face must have conveyed how sick I felt.

"On Friday, madam." I wished I could have said it better. I did not have the skill to cushion the blow.

Kate convulsed. There were no tears. She looked as though she might vomit. Her father took her hand and she drew in huge breaths, letting them out in jerky puffs. She stretched out her arm to me, something she would not normally do in front of her father, yet it was natural to go to her, take her free hand, and put my arm around her shoulders. Her convulsions gradually subsided into trembling.

"I am sorry I thought you might have betrayed your husband, Kate," Lord Sherbourne said. "I know that doesn't help at all, but still... I know you could not have done it."

A tiny spark of hope lit in my chest. Perhaps it did help. Not Edward, but Kate. If her father could be convinced that Makepeace had written the letter to the Bishop, he would withdraw his protection of the priest. Surely he would. But it was a long way from realising Kate did not want to be rid of her husband to being convinced that a man of God, in his family for twenty years, was a demon in disguise. My hope was tiny, yet perhaps it could be fanned into a flame.

I passed two days in a state of nervous tension. We did not leave *The White Hart* any more than we had to for fear of angry townsfolk. Lord Sherbourne paid the landlord extra money to prevent him asking us to leave. He also paid another visit to the justice, but returned shaking his head. There was no clemency, no commuted sentence, no mercy in this world. Our whole hope was for mercy in the next.

Ned was sent with a letter to Lady Sherbourne telling her what to expect, and she wrote back to her husband, ever the practical woman, to say she would visit the church to inform Reverend Smyth that a service was required. I wondered if he would refuse. Would he say that Edward should be buried at a crossroads like a suicide? But I did not dare ask out loud, even to Ned. I didn't want him to know I had such ghoulish thoughts. I would have to become a far better woman to be a good wife to him.

For the hundredth time, I sent up a prayer that Lord Sherbourne would see Makepeace had given Edward over to the law, and that he would rid us of his poison. If he did not, I would take it as a sign that my plan would not damn me absolutely. A life committed to being a good wife might weigh in my favour. Edward was not alone in needing mercy in the next world.

Lady Sherbourne also said she would tell Smyth to be ready to marry Ned and me as soon as possible. It would be a simple wedding – just a few words at the church door.

On Thursday, while Kate was visiting Edward again, Lord Sherbourne sent Ned to purchase a coffin and to hire a horse cart to carry it back home. Ned stowed them in the stables. I shuddered at the sight of it awaiting an occupant, one who was currently living and breathing.

Then it was Friday. No clemency was offered, not even that of the sentence being carried out behind closed doors. Kate had promised him she would be there. For her sake, he had not wished her to come, but she was determined. Therefore, I was determined too, although Ned was reluctant to let me. I reminded him that I would be his wife soon enough, but until then I would decide for myself.

Edward was the main attraction of the day. Excitement buzzed in the air. The pie men did a good trade. Soldiers and constables watched the people, weapons at their sides. Other men were already hanged in the town square. I began to doubt my decision. Kate faced away from them and ignored the pointing fingers. I followed her example.

They brought Edward out to jeers from the waiting crowd. The three days since I last saw him had taken their toll on him. His face was bruised. He was hatless and his hair was unkempt. He wore only his shirt and hose.

He faced the crowd before the low platform that had been built for him, found Kate's face and smiled painfully. Then he bowed stiffly to Kate's father and gave a small, sad wave of his hand to Ned and me.

A priest approached. One of the new sort, of course. Edward waved him away. The court clerk began to read aloud from his parchment. I saw his lips moving, at least. The crowd made too much noise for him to be heard, their excitement growing every moment. Amidst the shouts came sickening bursts of laughter.

I crept closer to Ned. He, his father, and Kate's father had removed their hats. Kate's chin trembled and she clung to her father's arm but she seemed in control, unlikely to faint away. My own face was wet.

The clerk finished speaking, rolled up his parchment, and waved a couple of constables forward. They moved in front of Edward and indicated that he should lie upon the wooden boards. Their politeness struck me as weirdly funny. A noise escaped my mouth that might have been a laugh and my hand flew up to put it back in. Ned's arm reached around my shoulders and pulled me towards him.

Edward kissed his hand toward Kate. Something golden winked from his hand. He gave the coins he held to the men, then laid himself on the narrow platform. His movements were stiff and slow – those of a man getting into bed at the end of a hard day's labour. One of the constables brought a sharp stone the size of his fist from the foot of Edward's wooden bed. I barely had time to wonder what he was going to do with it. He murmured to Edward, who shifted obligingly for the man to slip the stone into the curve of his back. Edward rolled back on top of it and winced. His chest heaved. His fingernails dug into the boards.

Now the men brought forward a thick door which had been leaning against a wall. The door was not a large one. Even I would have had to duck my head to enter through it. When they lay the door on top of Edward's body, he gave a great exhalation of air rather than a cry, and his face twisted into a grimace. It would have been a greater kindness to Kate to have found a larger one.

Edward's executioners brought large stones to place on top of the door, laying them in the middle and working outwards. I wondered if they worked fast out of pity or because Edward had paid them. His face strained in his efforts to breathe through gritted teeth.

The watching townsfolk grew strangely quiet. I peeked around Ned and saw faces riveted to the scene being played out, fascinated by the approach of death. So silent were they that I could hear Edward's shallow gasps. The constables grunted as they hefted the stones. Their boots scuffed the ground. Each new stone landed like a death blow.

Edward's skin grew paler. His teeth unclenched gradually and his eyes opened, wandering until they found Kate. He was turning blue. I could no longer hear any breath. His eyes gave one last flicker and then were fixed. His entire face relaxed and his jaw slipped open. Edward was dead.

In the crowd a baby cried, while silent tears coursed down the faces of the five people who loved Edward.

A subdued murmur crept around the people. By twos and threes, they slunk away – perhaps to go to church.

Ned and his father slipped away. I stood awkwardly, biting my lip, while Kate let her tears fall onto her father's cloak. They returned within minutes, driving the cart.

The constables began removing the stones while the coffin was brought down. Kate refused at first to be taken away from the scene. Lord Sherbourne looked over her head at me, imploring my help.

I put my hand gently on her back. "Madam, let me take you away. No good can come from staying. You have been brave – as brave as your husband. You have done your duty for now. When you have rested you will have strength for the next part. Please, come away."

She turned from her father and allowed me to support her to *The White Hart*. I ordered her a glass of wine and sat with her until Ned opened the door and let me know they were returned. It took me only ten minutes to pack the few belongings Kate and I had brought, and we left Rysham, taking Edward home at last.

CHAPTER SEVENTEEN

The streets were dead when we left the town. Everyone was at church. Thank goodness the people of Rysham were so religious, I thought wryly. Old Ned drove the cart behind Lord Sherbourne and Kate on horseback, and Ned and I brought up the rear. Kate wore a veil and sat wordlessly the whole journey.

She maintained her composure even through our village, where people were going about their business. Some crossed themselves as our procession passed. Men removed their hats. Everyone bowed their heads. Whatever their thoughts, Edward was still the landowner here. It was a relief to be amongst our own.

Lady Sherbourne and Jane came to the door. Makepeace appeared soon after, standing close behind them. A couple of servants' heads poked around corners before disappearing, no doubt to report to everyone else.

Kate went straight to her parlour, taking a crying Jane with her. While Ned and I dealt with the luggage and Old Ned went off to find some sturdy lads to help bring Edward into the house,

Lord Sherbourne spoke in a low voice to his wife and Make-peace. A change in his tone made me strain my ears to hear. Ned and I shared a darting look and then we cast our eyes back to the bags.

"He was not found guilty of that. He refused to plead. That means you *can* offer prayers for him, I think."

I heard Makepeace respond. "He is lost. Prayers will not save him."

"And yet," Lord Sherbourne said, "I expect you to offer them nevertheless."

He saw me dawdling with the bags and said, "Molly, let's have something to eat. I'm ravenous." Then he turned on his heel and went in.

The spark of hope ignited within me again when I heard Lord Sherbourne overrule Makepeace. If he would make him leave, we would be free of him with a clean conscience. Our new life would begin well.

I was encouraged in my hope when Makepeace made no more argument. Edward was brought into the chapel and Make-peace put on his vestments and led us in prayers for the dead. There was one person in the house he respected, or at least feared.

The next morning Reverend Smyth did not come to the house to lead us to church, and he made the funeral service short. A few villagers came to line the way but none saw Edward buried. He deserved better. I felt myself grow angry. Were we not meant to avoid judging others? I remembered then that I would have said some harsh things myself if I had not seen more than they had. These difficult months had changed many things. Besides, I had nothing to be proud of, knowing what I was capable of if Kate could not convince her father that Makepeace had sent the letter that killed Edward.

When Edward had been laid with his parents and Harry, we went home and got on with packing the things we would take with us and putting to rights everything we were leaving. The time for grieving would come, but not yet. This was a time for action. Kate steeled herself to it and if she was able, then so was I. Jane had shown herself capable of directing the maids while we were away, according to Lady Sherbourne, and she carried on now.

Ned and I were to be married on Monday morning, as soon as we could be after the Easter festivities. The day after we would lock up the house, say farewell to most of the servants, who had been paid off, and leave with just the few who wished to come with us. On Sunday evening, Kate held my hand when I went to help her undress.

"Do you look forward to it, Molly?" she said.

"Of course."

"Are you happy to be married this way? Now, I mean. It won't spoil your happiness?" Her face was lined with anxiety.

"Everything will be well. There is a new life about to begin and I would like to arrive into it a married woman."

Kate looked doubtful that I was content. I had some regrets, of course. It would not be the day I had imagined, a day of food and dancing, but that was not important. After all that had happened, it seemed frivolous to care about such things.

"I know your husband wished it, but that is not my only reason. I wish it too," I said. "He was right – our happiness can be snatched away. My greatest happiness is Ned. The sooner we marry, the better."

"And when we settle, we will celebrate properly," she said, squeezing my hand, "and welcome your little ones soon after that, I dare say."

I hoped so more than I could express in words. Instead of trying to say it, I squeezed her hand in return.

Our wedding was simple and more joyous than I could have hoped for. Reverend Smyth performed the ceremony well and even smiled to see how happy we were. Friends from the village came to wish us well. The women brought me posies of the first spring flowers from the meadows. The men shook Ned's hand and slapped him on the back, their wives pretending to scold them for their words of advice about that coming night.

Kate and her family watched us from a distance in their mourning clothes, allowing us to enjoy these moments. They brought Isabel too, who ran amongst the people and enjoyed them making a fuss of her. Margaret shadowed her but let her romp about. I caught Kate's eye several times but she did not make any move to hurry me. Makepeace's absence was the lifting of a menacing shadow that gave space for open laughter.

People began to trickle away and return to their work, and Ned and I left the churchyard in high spirits, following the family who had discreetly left ahead of us. The last of our friends stopped walking with us when we reached the boundary of the grounds. Ned and I wandered along, hand in hand, pausing before we reached the final bend in the path that would bring us in view of the house. He kissed me gently and stroked my cheek.

I hoped for a happy ending to all this – that Lord Sherbourne might discover the author of all the trouble, that the whole truth would reveal itself to him, and that he would save us all from Makepeace's vengeance. It happened in plays, I thought as I wrapped my arms around my husband's waist. Surely it could happen in life. Ned deserved the best wife. I wanted to be that wife.

I did not smile too broadly around the house that afternoon. Kate had been very kind to me. She did not deserve to be reminded that I had just gained a husband while she had lost one. Besides, my nerves were tightening again.

There was no more preparation for our departure that we could do. Our baggage was ready to load up the next morning. Lists had been checked, cupboards had been cleared, and only the things we would need for that night and in the morning were outstanding.

Ned had some matters to check with the horses and I reluctantly let him go. While I waited for him to be mine again, I wandered around the house, looked in through doors, opened drawers and chests and closed them again. The place seemed to know it was about to be abandoned and showed its displeasure in stony silence.

I came down the stairs for the second time in my wanderings, and the silence was broken by gradually rising male voices. I stood in the hall, wondering if I should venture along to the parlour, when the door of that room flew open and the muffled voices came into focus.

The first words I heard clearly were, "You will leave this instant."

My heart leapt. That was Lord Sherbourne. Carefully I crept to the parlour door.

He continued, "I have harboured you long enough! I might have believed your motives were good if you had told the truth. But you tried to blame the wife of the man you betrayed! You would have let us be ashamed of her. You would have let us believe she wanted to be rid of her husband."

My prayers had been answered. I rejoiced, but Makepeace did not look beaten. He stood squarely with Lord Sherbourne, less broad but taller.

"And she should have wished to be rid of him," said Makepeace. "Why else was his son taken but to punish him? Why else was he left with none but girls – one of them scarred and useless and the other an idiot who cannot be taught to behave? There was no hope for him."

Makepeace had lost his cool, superior air. His eyes flashed and spittle flew from his mouth as he talked.

"But women are weak vessels. They cry about *love* and such like." His face curdled in scorn. Lady Sherbourne, who had been attempting to get between the men, recoiled as he turned his face to her.

It was time to fetch help. I had to find Ned and make him step in, but I could not move my feet. Kate looked equally frozen in the corner of the room where she held Jane protectively in her arms.

"You will not find *me* weak," said Lord Sherbourne. "I don't care where you go. Slither back over the Channel, go to Hell as far as I care, but you will come along with me no longer. Your bag is packed. Take it and get out."

Lord Sherbourne grabbed him to force him through the door. Makepeace put his hands against the older man, but instead of grabbing him in return and pulling him closer, he gave him an almighty shove.

Lord Sherbourne was the stronger man, but Makepeace caught him off balance and he fell heavily to the floor. The hearth was behind him and his head struck the stone with a sickening thud. He lay still.

Jane screamed. The noise stirred me and I turned to run for help. I ran straight into Ned and followed him back into the room. Makepeace still stood firm, nostrils flaring. Ned judged his mood and gave him a wide berth, asking him by a gesture if he might leave the room. "Let the ladies tend to him, Father," he said.

Makepeace seemed to consider knocking down Ned too. A large part of me wished that he would try and do so. He would find himself on the wrong end of the business this time. But he had not lost his self-preserving judgement entirely, more's the pity. He stalked out of the room.

Lady Sherbourne was already at her husband's side. "Henry," she said. I had never heard her call him by his name. He was beginning to stir, and his wife helped him raise his head, her hand coming away bloodied.

At last I did something useful and ran to the hall where all the baggage had been stacked. I knew which trunk held the linen because I had packed it myself. Flinging open the lid, I grabbed the top pieces and ran with them back to the parlour.

Lord Sherbourne was sitting up, waving away his wife and complaining loudly. He demanded to know where *that damned priest* was and threatened to whip him like a dog if he was still in the house.

I peeked at the back of his head. The wound was seeping blood and I began tearing the linen into strips and placing them on the table. Kate folded and refolded one into a thick pad and placed it gently against her father's head. He winced, then reached behind and took it from her.

"Help me up," he said to Ned and offered up his free hand.

He stood briskly enough for a man of his age, but needed a chair put under him. He continued to swear about what he would do to Makepeace if he ever again clapped eyes on the man. I risked a look at Kate, which she understood. My relief and joy were reflected in her eyes.

We were free of him. He would have to find others who still believed his holy pretence in order to stay in the country. Preferably he would go further. I hoped he would not do too much damage wherever he ended up.

I went to find Lord Sherbourne something to drink. A single barrel stood in the kitchen and I filled a mug and took it back. His eyes were closed when I got back and he slouched in the chair.

"My Lord," I said quietly.

He opened his eyes and looked around himself as if confused to find himself in the parlour. I offered him the drink but he did not know what to do with it.

"Henry," said his wife again, sitting at his side. "You were thirsty."

He still did not take what I offered and closed his eyes again. His head lolled to one side. He slumped in the chair and both hands fell into his lap.

Kate, her mother and I exchanged glances.

"Henry, open your eyes." She sounded more her commanding self yet a note of fear had crept in below it.

His eyes opened again and there was something curious. One of them was normal but the other was... wrong. The blackness in the centre was wide, far wider than the other eye. The blue was almost eclipsed, as if a light had gone out.

Lady Sherbourne saw it too. I was glad that Kate did not.

It was too far to take him to his bed, even with Ned. And what good would it have done? Kate's mother held her husband in her arms as his breath grew fainter and fainter. After agonising minutes, Lord Sherbourne gave one final gasp and died.

CHAPTER EIGHTEEN

I woke exhausted from a fitful doze the next morning, still seeing Lord Sherbourne's broken eye in my mind. My hopes were dashed. The path ahead was fixed. I had not thought anything could be bad about sharing a bed with Ned, but I was terrified to sleep in case I talked. I could not bear for Ned to know his wife was a monster.

Ned stroked my arm and kissed my forehead. "Good morning, wife," he said. "You slept no better than I did, I think." I wanted to cry at how little I deserved the title or his kindness. A tear leaked out and he wiped it with his thumb.

"He was good, the old gentleman. And Father Make- ... the other man... will go abroad where he came from, let's hope."

More tears burst forth at that. Ned thought the best of people. He thought much better of them than I ever could. He thought I was grieving for Lord Sherbourne and I had to let him believe that I was as unselfish as that. My tears were for myself far more than for Kate's father, and Ned's sympathy deepened my guilt. A day married and already concealing truths from my husband.

I weighed my words carefully. "I wish I believed he would. But I think he may stay at the Manor a long time. I think he may bend the house to his own will." I began to speak faster, my words tumbling out. "He has already killed two men – what more will he do? He will make that place like a prison just as surely as he had Sir Edward locked up in one. We will all be his prisoners."

I stopped speaking abruptly. No more, before he guessed.

"Then we must leave our freedom – and his punishment – in the hands of God."

Oh, Ned, I thought. What freedom it must be to be a man, even though a servant.

We were leaving after breakfast so Ned was dispatched early to the village to bring back the best coffin our carpenter had in his workshop, with the order to say nothing about who had died.

"Let them all wonder and gossip for a while," Kate said. "It hardly matters any more."

Her mother looked as if she might disagree but changed her mind and shrugged.

At breakfast, Makepeace came into the dining room last and sat in Edward's seat at the head of the table. I stifled a gasp. Kate's father had sat there the evening before. He looked one by one at the three ladies around the table, challenging them to question his right. Jane appeared ready to cry again and slumped in her chair. Kate and her mother, although they were both pale, with red rings around their eyes, kept their attention on their bread and cheese. I wondered if they were as calm as they looked or if their hearts were leaping from their bodies like mine was.

Everyone wore travelling clothes in readiness for the journey, even to their boots. Everything else was either packed in trunks to come with us or wrapped up against the moths. Makepeace was also dressed to travel, with no hint of his profession about his appearance. I used to think of his layman clothing as his disguise, but his priest-clothes were the true disguise. There was no vocation in him. There never had been. He had always been a pretender.

Lady Sherbourne broke the silence. "Do you travel with us to the Manor, sir, or onward to your port?"

I held my breath. His answer was crucial. We might be able to take the path Lady Sherbourne preferred last night when she talked with Kate and me. Everything might be well. Perhaps. If only he would go.

Makepeace observed Lady Sherbourne insolently while he chewed his mouthful. He sat back in the chair and rested his arms as if he claimed ownership.

"I am undecided, madam. I may travel with you some distance and then leave on the Dover road, or I may attend you home and wait until summer before going back to the Continent. Or perhaps I will stay indefinitely. This bastard Queen cannot hold her throne forever. The Spanish will see to that. And when she is gone, I will be one of the first to benefit. The wheels of fortune turn so suddenly for all of us, don't you think?"

Lady Sherbourne listened to his entire speech without flinching. "Indeed, they do," she said. I did not need a look from her. The last faint hope was gone. Makepeace had sealed all our fates.

Lady Sherbourne had decided her husband's body would

wait for its burial preparation until we arrived at his own house. Our journey would be slow with the heavy carriage and laden carts and we had to bring him home before nightfall.

Ned and his father waited for me in Edward's study where Lord Sherbourne lay on the long table next to the coffin Ned had brought from the village. The luggage was all stacked outside the front door, except Makepeace's travelling bag. There was nothing left to do and so we could not put off this job any longer.

I brought with me a quantity of dried lavender and Ned had thrown the windows wide. The three of us silently wrapped Lord Sherbourne in a sheet and lifted him into his coffin with as much dignity as we could offer him. I scattered the lavender on top. The journey would take several hours at a cart's pace even if the roads were dry. Then Ned secured the lid. I hoped the work at the other end would be finished by the Sherbourne Manor servants.

When we were done, I nodded at the two strongest stable boys Ned had selected and who stood in the hall twisting their hats in their hands. They came in and positioned themselves at one end of the box, Ned and his father at the other. On Ned's command, all four lifted, then turned a shoulder underneath the coffin, settling the weight between them.

They processed solemnly out of the study, through the hall, and out the front door. Kate, her mother, and Jane followed them the short distance to where the cart waited to take Lord Sherbourne home. Isabel had been brought outside by Margaret, cloaked up and ready to step into the carriage. She stopped gambolling when her grandfather was brought out and glued herself to her nurse's side. Her doll hung lifeless from her hand.

From the doorway, I watched them load him up. It was not the ending the old man deserved, to be fitted in with the baggage, but we could do no more. When he was home, he would receive every honour. My bridal wildflowers were already wilting, but Lady Sherbourne placed them on his coffin.

The men melted away to finish their last few jobs with the horses. Lady Sherbourne turned her head, found me, and gave a single nod. It was time.

I turned to find Makepeace a few paces away, ready cloaked, and I gasped. Had he just come there?

"Sir, I will bring some drink into the parlour before we leave," I said. My voice trembled. I hoped I could pass it off as grief and as fright at his sudden appearance. My heart jolted into my mouth at the enormity of what we were about to do.

He stared at me, an amused curl to his mouth. For a moment, I thought he would refuse a drink before travelling just for the sake of opposing me. But he turned and went back to the parlour. His own self-interest was strongest. We depended on that being so. I breathed deeply to calm myself.

Kate had come back inside and saw his retreating back. She placed a reassuring hand on my arm and gave me a single nod just like the one her mother had given a few moments ago. Her own breathing was deep and deliberate too, though. I squeezed her hand gently to offer my comfort in return. She gave me a tiny smile.

I picked up the tray of ale mugs from the dresser and took a few more breaths until my hands shook less. Then I walked half a pace behind Kate into the parlour.

"I am surprised at you, madam," Makepeace said to Kate. She froze at his harsh tone. I froze behind her. I had the old, familiar feeling that he knew my thoughts. What if it was not my imagination? What if he really could hear what we were thinking?

"You chose *this* room to spend your last moments in this house? Where your father attacked me? Where God struck him down?" He gestured at the hearth and floor. It was wet and shining in all the places a maid had scrubbed it to remove Lord Sherbourne's blood.

Before, his words would have shamed me. I would have felt the judgement of Heaven. I had believed in his knowledge of God, even though I thought him a strange vessel for the Almighty to choose. But now, I heard his words for what they were – lies. Pure and simple – lies. He knew and cared only about his own benefit.

And so, instead of softening as I once would have, I felt my fear and nerves hardening into iron. I felt a resolve I had never felt before.

Quick footsteps sounded in the passageway. Lady Sherbourne. Makepeace's eyes went to the door. I am glad they did not fall on me. He might have seen the hatred I felt.

Kate's mother opened the door, bringing Makepeace's travelling bag. "Father, hide," she said. "There are soldiers. Quickly. Not a moment to lose." She closed the door behind her and continued talking fast at him.

I shoved the tray on the table and went to the section of panelling to the side of the chimneypiece. Kate helped me lift it and it came away smoothly. We put it to one side then Kate turned the key and flung the small door open wide.

All the while, Lady Sherbourne chattered away at him about the soldiers. How many there seemed to be, how fast they were riding, how this would finally be more than she could bear. She led him by the arm to the hole, glancing nervously at the door as if armed men would burst through at any moment. I was in awe of her.

She turned him to face into the room so he could lower himself to the floor and slide himself into his hiding place. Even as his legs obeyed, his expression was puzzled.

He slid into the gap. Then he brought his knees up and swung them in too. Kate moved forward and placed her hand on the door.

The door of the room opened. Jane ran in, calling out, "Mother, Isabel has fallen in the mud. What..."

Utter stillness took hold of the room. It lasted only a second and, at the same time, an eternity. That was all the time Makepeace needed to read the story on our faces. Jane's astonishment at the open priest hole said enough, but the guilt on every other face told him the rest. He bared and clamped together his teeth. His eyes flashed murder.

Kate moved to close the door on him. Once covered with the panelling, the noise he made would be muffled, I hoped. All we needed was to get out of the house. Everyone else was gone or ready to go.

She was not quick enough. While it was still half open, he flung his arm against the door, too strong for her, although she pressed her weight against it.

Jane was fastest. She hurled herself against the door, and together they gained ground. The gap narrowed by several inches. But they had no purchase against the damp floorboards, whereas Makepeace could move onto his knees and push hard off the stone wall. There was no room for me to add my weight to the door. I could only watch in horror with Lady Sherbourne as he forced the door open with a grunt like a boar. Kate and

Jane slid along the floor and his head and shoulders appeared. His face was red and mad.

"You bitches!" he roared, coming further into the room. "It'll have to be this way, then!" Jane's ankle was closest and he grabbed it. She screamed.

"You'll have to learn, all of you," he shouted, coming up from all fours onto his knees alongside Jane. He shoved Lady Sherbourne aside, come to shield her granddaughter, then brought his fist down into Jane's belly. She crumpled up and was silent, winded.

"That goes for you too, you old hag," he said over his shoulder. He was snarling now, about to deliver another blow to the girl on the floor, when Kate flung herself at him, her nails reaching for his face. She could not hold him off for long.

For a moment I considered running from the room, fetching Ned, anyone. But by the time I got back, what would he have done? And what would he do after?

I reached behind me. He was on one knee, Kate's wrists in his hands, pulling them away from his face. I was pleased to see blood oozing from his cheek, but soon he would be on his feet and it would be too late.

He shoved her away from him and she landed heavily against a table. He put a hand on the floor to regain his balance and moved his leg to stand up. This was my chance. I would not get another.

I brought the poker down hard on his skull. The crack brought a flash of the past into my mind, of when I was a girl and broke a serving bowl in two against the lip of the iron cooking pot. I gasped now as I did then.

His arms and legs gave way beneath him and his face struck the floorboards. He lay still. The wound above his ear pulsed out blood, already matting his hair. A red spray led back to the open hiding place like a trail of carnations.

I blinked at what I had done. Then I looked in turn at Lady Sherbourne, Kate and Jane. Each of them stared, open-mouthed. They really saw me for the first time in their lives.

CHAPTER NINETEEN

Three of us had chosen to murder him. But I alone had killed him. Kate and her mother were released from the guilt. They could leave me to bear it alone if they chose. They could let me face the punishment. They could even send for the constable themselves and have me hanged. Perhaps they would say I was driven mad by grief.

The moments stretched out. I looked from Kate, who still sat on the floor against the table where he had shoved her, to her mother, who stood with one arm flung out towards me.

In the end, Jane moved first. She inched towards his head, still holding her belly where he had hit her. Keeping her distance, as one would from a wild animal that might be merely stunned, she angled herself low down to see his face. From my position above him, I could not look away from the blood that seeped into his collar. The smell of it rose into the air, reminding me of the animal yard in autumn when the slaughterman had paid his visit.

Jane said, "He's dead."

The finality of her words unfroze us. I licked my lips and wondered whether I was going to vomit. Lady Sherbourne saved me from that.

"Molly, fetch linen," she said. "Quickly."

I had obeyed her since I was a girl. Doing as she told me was easy, even though I felt like I was in a dream, a nightmare. I stepped around the body towards the door. She took my wrist as I passed her and loosened the poker from my grip, then patted my arm to move me on.

I was soon back. Lady Sherbourne tore off some long strips of linen. She and Kate staunched the mess and packed Make-peace's collar with the fabric to keep the flow contained. Then we rolled him onto his back. His nose had broken a second time, but the blood did not concern me. I gasped when I saw how his eyes stared at me, though. They accused. Lady Sherbourne closed the lids.

"He cannot hurt you, Molly," she said. "He is a painted devil, that is all."

We did not have to drag him far – only a few feet. It was much harder to get him into the hole. He had been slender, but tall, and it took all our strength to shift and manoeuvre him through the gap. All the while the metal tang of his blood stuck in the back of my throat.

In the end, we had him slumped against the stone wall of the fireplace, his head resting against the wall of the passageway beyond. One leg twisted under him, the other bent up.

The four of us stood, panting with exertion. Blood stained my gown in patches and all of our trembling hands. It had dried in places. We cleaned ourselves as best we could with more strips of linen, then threw the soiled pieces through the gap. Kate picked up his travelling bag and placed that inside too, resting it at his feet. I was shaking in earnest now.

Then Kate stood at the open door to Makepeace's final resting place. "Are we done?" she said, looking for our agreement. All of us nodded at every other one of us. The pact was sealed. Kate closed the door and locked it. For a moment she hesitated, then removed the key, slid it into her pocket and patted the place where it weighed heavy in her skirt. Trembling, the two of us fitted the panelling to the wall. Jane and her grandmother straightened the furniture.

Kate took my hands in hers. She rubbed my fingers with her thumbs to comfort me. Jane joined us, taking one of my hands. Slowly, Lady Sherbourne came to stand with us too, and we held hands in a circle, all four of us. There was silence. I think that Kate's hand quivered a little, as did Jane's on my other side, but my own hands shook so violently that the movement might have been all my own. I had done a terrible thing.

My shaking lessened. Lady Sherbourne released the hands of her daughter and granddaughter, and straightened herself, poker-like. When she spoke, it was with quiet dignity.

"Your husband will have the horses ready by now," she said to me.

I bobbed a curtsey, although my knees still wobbled.

"And I must take my own husband home," Lady Sherbourne continued. "Katherine... Kate –" she said, "– it is time to leave." Then she encompassed us all in a commanding gaze. "Father Makepeace – my cousin, Mister Farendon, I should say – has travelled on ahead to find a ship," she said. "He has chosen his own path."

She nodded at the cloaks, gloves and mourning veils on the table. I dropped the hands which still held mine and scurried to fetch them. It was an everyday task I had done for them many times and performing it calmed me further. I was still their Molly.

Once I had helped the ladies with theirs, Kate helped me put on my own cloak and gloves. They covered the bloody spots on my dress and hid the staining on my hands. I could wash later. We all could.

We left Kate's parlour for the last time, along the passageway and through the hall. I had no doubt the house would stand empty for some time – people still believed in ghosts and curses for all the church preached against it. Edward's infamy would save us. Perhaps the house might be happy again in time, when the stench of rot had decayed to dust, but for me – and Kate and Jane and Lady Sherbourne, it held nothing we cared to remember.

Isabel was singing outside. Ned peered curiously at me from the threshold. I smiled at him. A new life beckoned. I was determined to do all I could to deserve a happy one.

Ned stood back to allow Lady Sherbourne to pass through the door. Kate paused to lift the huge door key from its hook, and then she and Jane went outside. As I left the house and stepped into the light, I noted with admiration that not one of them trembled. And nor would I.